Falling for Her First Love

Port Provident Holiday Hearts

Kristen Ethridge

<u>Chapter One</u>

Chapter One

NOTHING LOOKED OUT of place. Even the slightly worn Columbia-blue-and-white linoleum tiles covering the hallway of Port Provident High School didn't appear any different than when Meg McMahon last stepped down the corridor.

More than ten years had flown off the calendar, but less than a week back in town made Meg feel as though she'd walked back into a time warp. To the untrained eye, time had not moved on. But Meg knew that to be a lie. She'd last walked down this hall on her graduation day. Just a few hours later, she'd gotten married in a whirlwind trip to the justice of the peace one county over. Port Provident's favored son, the star, the all-state quarterback, Dan Clark, had turned a child from a badly broken home into a fairy tale princess. He'd taken her from the ashes and made her Cinderella.

But everyone knew fairy tales weren't real. And apparently, neither was Dan Clark's love.

Meg tried to focus on the mission at hand and keep the memories at bay. She just needed to bring Lamont's medical clearance form to the trainer. As she stepped out of the main high school building and walked down the back sidewalk at the edge of the student parking lot, she formulated a plan.

She would just duck inside the field house and lay the single sheet of paper on the trainer's desk. Thinking back to

the layout of this building, Meg knew it wouldn't be hard to run in and run out—assuming that, like the high school itself, the field house probably hadn't changed much either. In those years when she was Dan Clark's one-and-only, Meg had often been by his side while he got his ankle taped or got checked after practice. She knew right where the trainer's room was. She wouldn't need to get anywhere near the field where her ex-husband —now the head football coach at Port Provident High School—was conducting a practice for this week's season-opening game.

Meg pulled open the heavy metal door on the side of the squat, windowless building. Olfactory memory jumped front and center. She knew this smell. Most people would write it off as sweat and gym socks. Instead, Meg remembered hard work, dedication, and dreams. She'd never stepped on a field, but they'd been her dreams too. Her dreams for her future with Dan had been all wrapped up in football.

"Can I help you?"

Meg stopped, but couldn't turn to face the man who called to her.

Even her toes curled under with the instant recognition.

It was the boy her mama had warned her about.

Well, Trudy had technically been her aunt and the boy was now a man. But, as Trudy predicted more than a decade ago, Dan *had* ultimately broken Meg's heart.

And as that poor, wounded heart pounded in her chest, Meg knew she wasn't as over the events as she'd hoped.

She knew she should turn around. She knew she should reply to the well-intentioned question. But she couldn't.

The sound of footsteps on the concrete floor came closer.

And then it happened. Two fingers lightly tapped her on the shoulder. The touch she'd dreamed about for almost ten years.

Meg sighed slightly, wishing that the casual graze across the top of her T-shirt sleeve meant the security it had once signaled to her. Not this heart-thumping, sticky-sweating, feeling of fear and anxiety.

Slowly, she turned and looked into the eyes of her past.

"Meg?" Dan's whisper echoed in the stark hallway. "What are you doing here?"

"This." She stuck Lamont's form out and took one step back, not trusting herself to be close enough to touch or to speak more than a single syllable. He wouldn't reach out again, she knew—he never had—not even once—since he cut her out of his life.

She also didn't trust herself not to slap him silly. He deserved one open-palmed paddle across the cheek for every sleepless night she'd had since leaving the cramped collegiate apartment they'd called their own.

Dan took the page from her outstretched hand, grabbing the corner diagonally across from where Meg's hand held on. She felt thankful for the distance. Even eight-and-a-half-by-eleven inches of paper seemed like protection right now. She would take what she could get.

"Lamont Brown's medical clearance? Why do you have this?" Dan's head cocked at a slight angle.

"He's staying with Trudy." She wanted to keep things as simple as possible right now. They'd been complicated enough for so long.

Dan nodded, still fixing her with that pinching stare. "I know that. Are you staying with Trudy?"

Meg released her hold on the paper and watched the corner float downward. She didn't want to look Dan in the eye anymore. The weight of his stare continued to push on her. "Yes."

"After all this time? Why? I know she's asked you before to come...home." He lingered on that last word. Maybe he remembered telling her that he'd be her forever home as he slipped the chip-sized diamond engagement ring on her finger after the homecoming football game.

"She wasn't recovering well from her knee surgery, and she's got a few big catering jobs in the next few weeks. She needed help. I couldn't say no."

Losing her job last week made it convenient to say yes to Trudy's most recent request to return to Port Provident. Nothing made it easy.

And the reason why stood right in front of Meg.

"Are you staying long?"

Meg wondered why he asked. "Why? Do you need to calculate how long to avoid me? You've been practicing that for a while. You didn't even tell me you were leaving. Just wrote a letter telling me *they* said you needed to cut some ties." No matter what, at least she knew she wouldn't cry in front of Dan. She'd let go of her last tear for him before she even turned twenty.

All subsequent tears had rained solely for herself.

Or so she'd thought.

"Coach! You coming?" A ray of sunlight cut through the dimness in the corridor as the heavy door to the field opened.

A kid, dressed for practice in full pads, stood in the doorway. "Coach Brumley said he needs to ask you something about the drills."

"Yeah, Reese. I'm comin'." Dan ran an open palm down the side of his face and wiped his chin. Meg knew it would feel faintly of five o'clock shadow, even though it was barely three in the afternoon.

She'd known everything about him, before...

Watching his simple gesture got the best of her resolve. Memories prickled across her fingertips, drawing the mental imprint of a sandpaper rasp beneath them. Meg wedged her hand into the tight jeans pocket just below her hip, trying to erase the feeling with the rub of denim.

"Can you just see that the trainer gets that?" She inclined her head toward the paper in Dan's hand. "Trudy said it was important for Lamont."

His dark hazel eyes were distant—not intent like they had been only moments before. Part of her wanted to know what he was thinking. The other part reminded her that what she didn't know couldn't really hurt her.

"Yeah, he needs this to be able to play this season." Dan turned to walk outside, then stopped abruptly. "Will you be there?"

Once upon a time, she'd always been there for Dan. Because he'd always been there for her. But then, one day, he left.

She stood there without answering until Reese shouted again. "Coach?"

His breath released and the muscle at the back of his jaw locked into place. He pulled his gaze back and caught Meg's

glance with a determination that she hadn't seen since that last state playoff game.

"Yeah, Reese. I'm comin'," he said.

And then, once again, Dan Clark walked away without another word.

AS SOON AS DAN STEPPED onto the sidelines of the Port Provident High School football practice field, twenty different voices called at least as many different questions in his direction.

But all he could hear was the silence where Meg's answer to his question should have been. He should have known Meg wouldn't want anything to do with him or Port Provident football. She said she came back to town as a favor to Trudy. She dropped off the medical form as a favor to Lamont.

Meg didn't owe Dan any favors. That much he knew. Not after the way he treated her. He'd asked God for forgiveness for his actions, but he'd never been brave enough to ask Meg.

He didn't deserve her forgiveness.

"Dan? You look like you've seen a ghost." Zack Brumley rapped his best friend on the arm with the clipboard he faithfully carried.

Dan stood, arms crossed, watching the players start their drills. "Meg's back."

A whistle tweeted at the other end of the field.

"Meg McMahon?"

Dan's head whipped around involuntarily. "Clark." He spit out the correction, but he didn't know why it mattered to him.

Zack watched one of his linemen make a tackle. "Not like that, son. Get your head up and look at what you hit. Otherwise, that's a good way to wind up on a stretcher."

His fellow coach never took his eyes off the field. "You've got about as much sense as that boy out there."

"*Hmph.*" Dan knew Zack was right, but he didn't really feel like admitting it.

"You think she kept your last name after everything?" Zack kept watching practice, attempting disinterest.

"I've got to go give Lamont Brown's release to Mitch." Dan needed to get away from Zack's laconic correctness.

Dan tried to watch what was happening on the field as he walked to the far end of the sideline where Mitch Sullivan, the head trainer for the Port Provident Pirates, stood. But he couldn't. All he could think about was running into Meg.

Here.

In Port Provident.

At the field house.

At *his* field house.

He wondered where she'd been all this time. It didn't take long for him to realize the hangers-on of the Lone Star University football program had filled his head with bad advice. But for Meg's sake, he never tried to find her. She'd deserved to rebuild her life without a fool like him.

And from what he saw today, she'd been doing well. She still had that same petite frame with curves in all the right places and her auburn hair framed her face in a long, wavy style he'd seen on one of those "America's Sweetheart"-type of actresses in a recent movie.

He remembered back to a time when Meg had been *his* sweetheart. Her shy presence gave him confidence when a hundred people across the country wanted something from him. As a highly recruited quarterback, the list of collegiate coaches who wanted him to listen to the virtues of their programs seemed to never end. And right behind them came the line of people who wanted something of Dan's success for themselves.

But not Meg. She didn't like the spotlight. She never asked Dan for anything he couldn't give.

And true to form, once again he saw her quietly standing at the edge of the chain link fence, studying the practice field. It looked like she'd never left, like time hadn't passed since she last watched him prowl the lines on this grass. She met his gaze, then scurried off like a spooked deer on the side of one of the sleepy Texas Hill Country highways that wrapped around Lone Star University—where their dreams had both come together and diverged almost simultaneously.

Dan stopped and watched her. He didn't know what the emotion was rising in his chest. Was he glad to see Meg again, or would he—like she predicted—avoid her until she left town?

He needed a game plan. Dan looked at the clipboard in his hand, marked up with Xs and Os. He knew all about game plans. He'd taken this football team to the state semi-finals last year on the strength of his strategies.

As he watched his ex-wife climb in a compact, four-door Mazda at the edge of the parking lot, Dan Clark drew up another quick plan: he would not fumble her heart again. And that meant he had to give her a wide berth while she was in town.

He scanned the sideline again and headed back in Mitch's direction.

Focus on the game, Clark. She'll be gone soon enough. Just keep staying out of her way until then.

"DID YOU GET LAMONT'S form turned in?" Trudy called from her swing on the front porch.

Meg stuffed her keys in the small pocket at the back of her purse as she walked up the steps to the Victorian house in the heart of Port Provident.

"Yes, it's taken care of." She wished she could say the same about her heart. It hadn't slowed down since she first heard Dan's voice in the field house hallway.

Trudy pointed at the white wicker chair next to the swing. "Have a seat. You've been running every minute since you got back to Port Provident."

Sinking into the tufted red-and-white striped cushion atop the chair, Meg finally relaxed a bit. It felt good to be cradled in something soft. "There's just lots to do before the Bassett anniversary dinner tonight."

"I know, but it'll all get finished." Trudy patted Meg's hand. "I'm sorry that chain bought out the hotel you worked for and reorganized you out of a job. But on the other hand, I'm so glad it happened and gave you the opportunity to come back home. I've missed getting to see you the last few years. You worked so many hours, I didn't get to spend much time with you on my trips to Austin. And I know your culinary skills will be a treat for my clients."

"*Mmm-hmm.*" Meg barely noticed the touch of Trudy's hand.

"You saw him, didn't you?"

"Huh?" Meg turned to look at Trudy. "Who?"

"Dan Clark. You ran into him up at school, didn't you?" Her great-aunt Trudy had been the only real mother Meg had ever known, and her instincts still worked even now that Meg had been an independent adult for years. "I hoped that since practice time had already started, he'd be otherwise occupied."

"He was leaving the field house just as I walked in." Meg wanted to tell Trudy about how her heart raced at the sight of Dan, but she knew she couldn't. Back in the days when everyone said girl with an unstable childhood would be a bad influence on the high school superstar, only Trudy spoke differently. Only Trudy said it would be the other way around.

Trudy said Dan Clark would break Meg's heart.

The events of a decade ago showed Trudy's hunch to be a good one. How could Meg tell her now that as shocking as seeing Dan had been, something deep inside had fluttered with the same excitement she'd felt when she was naïve and eighteen?

For once, she couldn't come clean to Trudy.

"Well, I'll be back on my feet soon, and you'll head back to Austin to look for a new job. With everything going on here between the weddings and the gala at Provident College, it shouldn't be too hard to stay out of his way for a couple of weeks." Trudy leaned forward and sat her empty glass on the small end table that stood just off the edge of the swing. "Can you hand me those crutches, dear?"

Guilt crept up and nudged Meg as she handed the crutches to Trudy. She'd always been able to tell Trudy anything because she knew her great-aunt would unfailingly keep her confidences. Trudy knew the one secret the rest of Port Provident did not. And whether or not Trudy agreed with Meg's reasoning to keep it hush-hush for the last ten years, she never breathed a word. Not at her sewing circle, not at her Bible study, and not in her afternoons when she used to wait tables at Porter's Seafood along Gulfview Boulevard.

Trudy was more than just the mother figure in Meg's life. She was the one person who'd never let her down.

"Will you head upstairs and double check that I pulled out the right table linens for tonight? Oh, and I hate to ask this, but can you straighten up Lamont's room a bit? It smells a bit like teenage boy and sneakers when you get to the top of the stairs." Trudy's crutches made clicking noises with every small step she took. "I'll limp around the kitchen a bit and double check that all the dishes are ready to go in an hour."

At first glance, Lamont's room, off the back of the upstairs landing, looked like a good space for a teenager to call his own. A quilt featuring a navy-and-Columbia blue pirate silhouette on a white background covered the bed. A few pillows in complimentary colors leaned back and obscured most of the headboard. A small student desk with a few drawers and an older wooden chair took up residence under the window at the back of the room. Some papers were scattered across the top. A pair of tennis shoes sat at the end of the bed and a solitary gray

T-shirt streaked with sweat stains was tossed carelessly over the top of another chair near the closet.

Nothing seemed out of the ordinary. But Meg could see something was missing. Something important. Personal possessions.

No snapshots in frames lined the bookshelf, no collectibles sat out with pride, no piles of a teenage wardrobe casually heaped in the corner. Not even a well-worn stuffed animal saved throughout the years could be seen.

Foster kids didn't bring much with them from home to home.

Just their hopes for the future. And often times, there wasn't even enough of that to bring along.

Meg remembered the day when she came to Trudy's house after the death of her grandmother. After Meg left, Trudy declared the house too quiet and went through formal certification to be a foster parent. Ten years of children had been loved since then.

She couldn't see much to tidy up, as Trudy asked—Lamont had even made his bed before heading to school this morning—so Meg attacked the few items in plain sight. She plucked the shirt off the chair back and placed it in the hamper, and moved the shoes inside the closet.

Meg stopped at the desk and started to organize the scattered papers into a neat pile. Picking up the white sheets, she couldn't help but notice a bright yellow sticky note affixed to a page of recent math homework. Hastily scribbled on the small square was a name and phone number which began with an Austin area code.

Barry Haynes.

Liquid electricity surged through her veins. In one swift motion, she peeled the sticky note off the other page. Errant corners poked into her palm as she crushed the note in her hand.

Meg hadn't officially met Lamont Brown yet. But she knew there was no way she was going to let slick-talking Barry Haynes ruin one more vulnerable kid's life. He'd already come dangerously close to ruining her own life a long time ago. At that time, she'd been paralyzed by the fear Barry put in her. She'd just done what she'd been told and kept quiet. He told her it would be better for her that way. She'd recognized the threat when she heard it.

Meg grabbed her keys and took off running for her car.

Chapter Two

THE CHAIN MAIL FENCE behind him kept rattling. It sounded like another hurricane decided to bear down on Port Provident. Dan gave two chirps of his whistle to signal to the team that it was time to run sprints, then turned around.

It wasn't a tropical cyclone, but the sight at the fence was equally full of fury.

"Meg?"

She pressed a yellow sticky note against the fence. "How dare you, Dan? You're still hanging out with this guy?"

Dan walked toward the fence, then stood back as the scribbles on the note came into focus.

"I haven't talked to Barry in years, Meg."

Her eyes flashed with fury that reminded Dan of something found in one of the circles described in Dante's *Inferno*. "Then how does he know Lamont Brown?"

Dan lifted his cap, pushed back his hair with one hand, then put the cap back down and adjusted it on his forehead.

"I don't know, Meg."

"I don't believe that for a minute. You've had a relationship with Barry Haynes for years. Now you have a relationship with Lamont Brown. The common denominator is *you*."

"I don't have a relationship with Barry, Meg."

"That's rich—you know, like you thought you were going to be if you just listened to Barry's slick advice, Mr. NFL Quarterback." She wrinkled her nose as though someone had just opened a trash can in her presence. "Speaking of relationships, I've always blamed Barry Haynes for the end of ours, so forgive me for not trusting him—or a single word you say."

Dan shoved his fist into his pocket. "Look, Meg. I'm not asking you to trust me. I'm just asking you not to start throwing blanket accusations in my direction."

She took a step back from the fence. The high color in her face lingered.

"Fine," she said, pressing her lips together forcefully as the one syllable escaped. "Do me one favor, though."

"What?" It surprised Dan a little to realize that he still wanted to make Meg happy.

"Keep Barry away from Lamont. Keep Barry away from your program."

"I swear I haven't seen him in years. But I'll get to the bottom of it. And I'll talk to Lamont."

Meg reached behind her head and tightened her hair where it hung in a long ponytail. She'd highlighted it. The variety of shades woven into the strands suited her.

"Thank you," she said.

"But can you do me a favor in return?" This might be the last time Meg would ever speak to him. He needed to make the most of the chance.

The curve of her eyebrow shifted to a more pronounced point. Her reply was more grunt than an actual word. "Huh?"

"Come to the game Friday night."

"I'm busy."

She answered far too quickly for Dan's preference. The speed with which her words shot out indicated she hadn't even given it any thought.

Not for one single second.

He knew that although she'd answered, it wasn't *the* answer. She was holding something back. Even after all this time, Dan still knew Meg. He still could read her quirks.

He wished he could read her mind.

Or maybe not.

There were probably a lot of unflattering words going through her head right now, and they would all be connected directly with his name. Dan probably didn't need to know *exactly* what Meg thought of him. He could get the general gist just by looking at the expression on her face. The pointy eyebrow had now been joined by a slight snarl of the right side of her upper lip.

Nevertheless, he wasn't going to let her just walk away again. He'd let other people make his decisions once upon a time.

Now, he stood on his own two feet.

And this time, those two feet were going to stand firm.

"How 'bout I leave you some tickets at will call in case your plans fall through?"

Her lips twitched in disapproval again, and she shot back another quick answer. "I doubt they will."

"Well, you never know. Sometimes, things change, Meg. Actually, everything does...eventually." Dan looked down at his watch. Although he needed to get through to Meg, his kids also needed their coach to get back to practice. "The tickets will be there if you change your mind. You should come watch Lamont. He's a really gifted player. He's got a shot at going all the way if he stays disciplined and coachable. He's got the natural talent. You'd be impressed."

"Trudy said that too. That's why you have to keep Barry away from him. Please."

Dan heard pain in that last word, and he knew he'd put it there. She'd been carrying that pain for ten years.

"I gave you my word, Meg." He had to say it. He had to. He needed to have the last word here. "Please give me yours and come to the game."

She took a deep breath. "Fine. For Lamont."

"OKAY, THAT SHOULD DO it." Meg placed an electric bill from Trudy's house on the registrar's desk. She could feel her hand cramping slightly from filling out several pages of school registration forms.

"Thank you, Ms. McMahon. Let me go make some copies and I'll bring back your originals."

Meg sat on the bench in the front office at Port Provident Elementary School.

"I'll make friends here, right?" Liquid brown eyes stared straight at Meg like a warm chocolate chip cookie straight out of the oven.

"Sure you will. You're a great kid. I know it's hard to be uprooted like this, but Trudy needed us. You'll be back with everyone in Austin soon." Meg took the young girl's hand in her own. "Besides, no matter what, you're my best friend. Never forget that. You've always got a friend. Me."

Ellie kicked at her hot pink backpack. "I'm not sure that's going to make me cool."

"Probably not. But it does make you loved." Meg put an arm around Ellie's shoulder and squeezed.

Brenda Campbell, the registrar, came back around the corner and handed back the papers to Meg. "We'll put Ellie in Miss Sanderson's class. There are some nice girls in there, so I'm sure she'll get to know everyone quickly. Would you like to walk with us to the classroom, Ms. McMahon?"

Meg looked down at Ellie. "Sure...I mean...maybe not. Ellie's in fourth grade. It's probably cooler if I don't come. Cool's the thing, right, Ell?"

Ellie smiled. Meg could see the one slightly crooked eye tooth poking out. "It's definitely a thing."

The registrar led the way out of the front office. As soon as they stepped into the main hallway, the volume increased significantly. But the voices Meg heard definitely weren't elementary voices.

"Coach, you can take the team into the cafeteria and get them lined up on the stage. We'll start bringing in all the kids for the assembly in about fifteen minutes." A woman in athletic wear pointed to a door down the hall.

Meg saw a ball cap in the crowd and froze.

She definitely wasn't surrounded by elementary schoolers. The hallway was jam-packed with high school football players.

Specifically, Dan Clark's high school football players.

Her hands cupped around her nose and mouth, and Meg could hear the sound of her breathing. Her lungs pushed air in and out at a rate that was easily three times faster than her normal pace.

Oh, please God...not Dan. Just keep Ellie in the reeds, God. Just keep her in the reeds. Meg's hasty prayer of a decade ago flooded back as though she still prayed it every day. In the early days, Meg asked God for protection, that she'd be so far off Dan's radar once she left his life that he couldn't take everything away from her ever again.

And Ellie was everything to her. Of all the things in her life, only Ellie mattered.

"Miss Sanderson!" Brenda Campbell called out over the commotion all around. At the sound of her strong voice, everyone turned and looked her way. "I was just bringing you a new student. This is Ellie Clark."

Meg stopped breathing. Her head began to swim. A little to the left, a little to the right...

She had to keep it together. She couldn't fall. She was the only protection Ellie had.

Along with the attention of all the visitors from Port Provident High School, Dan's head turned and followed the sound of the registrar's voice.

Floating gray spheres began to dance at the corners of Meg's vision. *Breathe, Meg. You have to breathe.* She forced air through the fingers still laced around the center of her face.

Meg saw Dan looking at the tall fourth-grader shaking hands with her new teacher. His head swiveled to the right and Meg knew Ellie was now in his line of sight.

Before Ellie had ever been born, Meg prayed that there would be figurative reeds to surround Ellie like the real ones had surrounded Moses in the Bible—giving him the protection he needed from the Egyptian soldiers while he waited in his basket to be noticed by Pharoah's sister. Meg had done everything she could for nine-and-a-half years to protect Ellie.

But now, the reeds parted, revealing the jewel in Meg's life, her most closely-guarded secret—the reason she not only walked away, but never looked back.

Dan's eyes widened as he took in the dark, shoulder-length hair and the dark eyes, fringed by thick black lashes. Meg knew he had to feel as though he were looking in a mirror.

She saw his reflection every time she looked at their daughter.

All the boys on the football team resumed their conversations. The volume level in the hall quickly reached a fever pitch once again.

But for Meg McMahon and Dan Clark, time stood still between them in the corridor.

Then, Eleanor Danielle Clark tucked a lock of hair behind her ear and waved bravely to her mother as she headed down the hall alongside her new teacher, oblivious to the fact that her life would never be the same again.

"GUYS, GO IN THE CAFETERIA and get on stage. Sit on the risers until the kids come in." The weight of more than fifty pairs of eyes on the back of Dan's head fell on him more heavily than anything available to his athletes for lifting in the fieldhouse workout room. "Go. Now."

Two short claps got the football team's attention. For close to twenty years, Zack Brumley had proven time and again that he had Dan's back. Never had Dan been more grateful for his friend than right now. "Come on guys, let's get ready for the rally. Cortland and Watson, grab those boxes of posters and pocket schedules," Coach Brumley said.

The hallway cleared out quickly, leaving only Dan and a wave of emotions...and Meg.

He knew what he'd seen in that girl's eyes, he knew what he'd heard when she'd been introduced to the teacher. But he couldn't wrap his mind around it. It just didn't make any sense.

"Meg." Dan could barely get his ex-wife's name past the lump in his throat. He clutched at her arm, letting action do the talking instead. He'd never preferred talking anyway—he'd been playing football and taking action since he was a kid.

He saw steel in Meg's eyes.

He saw flame.

And once again, he saw fear. Fear of him.

Meg's nostrils flared, taking in extra quantities of oxygen. It didn't take much observation to notice that everything about her was on heightened alert. The amount of adrenaline dumping into her veins had to rival a championship game with everything on the line. Everything in her body said flight.

But Dan was determined to stay and fight.

He was going to fight for Ellie Clark—whoever she was.

Scratch that. There wasn't any mystery around who Ellie Clark was.

He was going to fight to find out why he hadn't been told he had a daughter.

"I'm not wrong, am I?"

The woman with whom he'd once shared everything in his life shook her head.

"What's her name? Ellie?"

"Eleanor Danielle." Meg turned her head and looked down the hallway where their daughter had followed her new teacher to class. "She's named for her dad."

Meg's voice dropped so low, Dan almost missed the last part. But it shot an arrow straight into his erratically beating heart. "I have a daughter? And you named her for me?"

"Yes," she said with the flatness of the surf before sunrise.

"But you didn't tell me about her?"

"No."

"Why not, Meg?" Dan couldn't stop the words from coming out on a wave of volume. He knew he was yelling, but he didn't care. He couldn't control it. Shock had given way to anger. "I have a daughter who's what—ten years old—and you never thought to send me so much as a Christmas card to let me know?"

Glassy shards of light circled the irises of her gray eyes. "It's complicated. And she's nine. Almost nine-and-a-half."

"Nuclear physics is complicated, Meg. Telling your husband he has a child is not."

"You're my ex-husband, Dan. *You* filed for divorce, remember? I never heard from you again after that day."

He let go of her elbow and waved his hands in frustration. "Well maybe I wouldn't have if I'd have known. Meg, you never even gave me a chance."

She leaned forward, so close that she'd definitely crossed into his personal space. "Don't you dare go revising history, Daniel. *You* never gave *me* a chance. *You* never gave *us* a chance. Slick Barry Haynes filled your head with a bunch of pie-in-the-sky about NFL contracts and endorsement deals and how you'd be more marketable if you were a good-looking single guy with a cannon for an arm and the world at his feet."

Dan stepped back from Meg's white-hot rapid-fire. The words slapped him in the face with more force than even the nastiest sack he'd ever taken on the field. He'd been knocked unconscious during a game more than once.

But never had Dan been knocked back a decade in time.

He'd heard Meg's words before. Barry Haynes had walked with him around campus one fall day and explained to him that he could go number one in the NFL draft. Teams wanted him. They wanted to build franchises around the tight spirals he could throw and his deadly accuracy for finding receivers inside the red zone. Advertisers wanted him to sell their products. They wanted everything about Dan Clark except a teenage marriage with a girl from the wrong side of the tracks.

He looked back in his ex-wife's eyes and saw smoke.

Smoke and mirrors.

That's what Barry Haynes had sold him.

Because three years later when he tore every ligament in his left leg so badly that rehabilitation and a comeback wasn't even an option, everything he'd been promised was gone.

And so was Meg.

And so, apparently, was the daughter he never even knew he had.

"How did you know Barry said all that to me?"

Meg tilted her head, her hair slipping over her shoulders like a waterfall. "Said it to *you*? That's word for word what he told me the day he delivered your letter saying you wanted a divorce."

Dan wanted to be mad at Meg so badly. "So why didn't you tell me, Meg? I deserve an answer to that."

"I told Barry. That should have been enough. The two of you were thick as thieves back then. Your parents hired him to be a private coach for your added development, but you were his ticket to the big time. He was going to get to be an agent and live the good life—all he had to do was deliver Dan Clark to the right team at the draft."

"Wait—you told Barry?" Dan jumped in between her acid-tinged words.

"I did."

"But you didn't tell me?"

She swallowed hard. Dan watched the muscles in her throat contract in order, from jaw line to collarbone. He could have reached out a finger and traced the path. He wanted to. Something about Meg still pulled him in, even in the midst of this whirling fury.

Meg raised a shoulder. "He put money in an account for Ellie. He said he'd pay for her college and the rest of my studies...if I just walked away and never contacted you again. If I did contact you or contest anything, he would take it all back. We'd been married for two years, but I hadn't had a meaningful conversation with you in six months. It was all about you and your dreams and your future. There was no longer an 'us' and I knew it. I was getting ready to be a twenty-year-old single mom with no family, no support, and no prospects. I didn't have any choice other than to take Barry up on his offer—or to get rid of my baby, and I wasn't doing that. Not for you, not for him, not for anyone."

She bit her lip and looked back down the fourth-grade hallway.

Dan took an uneasy breath. Shame washed over him. He couldn't even look at Meg. The anger he wanted to feel betrayed him and ran away.

Just like he'd betrayed Meg and run away for something he'd been convinced would be better.

"That's why you've got to keep him away from Lamont, Dan. Lamont doesn't have any support either. I won't see his life ruined by Barry's fast talk."

Dan knew now there was no way he could atone for the past, but he could make sure he didn't break any more promises. "I told you I would, Meg. I mean it."

Slowly, he raised his hand, and with one finger, cut through the distance between them. A shock like static flashed across the swirls of his fingerprint as he touched it to Meg's chin and pressed the direction of her face back toward him.

Once again, his throat physically closed. He had to push through and get the words out, even though he had no right to. But he'd sworn to himself just a few moments ago that he would fight for Ellie Clark.

"Can I meet her, Meg?" The enormity of the question almost brought him to his knees. Although he'd been a competitor his whole life, never had he wanted a victory so badly.

Dan looked in Meg's eyes, wanting to find something in them to steady himself. Would she say yes?

A cheer erupted from the cafeteria as the elementary students filed in to meet this year's football players and get a free ticket to tomorrow night's game. But that was the only noise around them. Meg remained silent.

"Meg," he said, almost in a whisper. "I want to meet her. I don't know if I deserve to, but I want to. I don't even know how, but I'll beg if you want me to. But, please. She's my baby."

Her face remained expressionless. "I don't want you to beg, Dan. I don't want anything from you. I held to my end of the bargain. I haven't asked for anything for ten years now."

Suddenly, Meg's face flashed with light. A smile broke her lips into the generous curve he'd once loved to tease with kisses. Meg waved, and Dan saw a dark-haired girl in line wave back.

He blatantly stole as long of a look as he could. It might be the only one he ever got of his only child.

Then he stole a look at Meg too, her entire expression lit with love. It might be the only chance he ever had to see that look again—even if this time, that look wasn't for him. It used to be, and heavily, Dan realized he missed it.

"I'll bring her to the game tomorrow night," Meg said. "But it's up to her. The only thing I've ever done since I signed the papers Barry brought me was to try and protect her. Right or wrong, she's come first in my life since that day. That doesn't change just because you're in the picture now, Dan. Whatever she chooses to do is her decision and you and I are both going to respect it."

Then, just like so many years ago, Meg was gone. But this time, Dan was old enough to know what he'd lost.

Chapter Three

MEG NEEDED SOME PEACE. And some coffee.

She turned off the radio in her car, rolled down the driver's side window, and headed downtown to get a jolt of caffeine. She was alone with nothing except too many of her own thoughts. As she passed by street corners and houses she remembered from her youth in Port Provident, a certain type of nostalgia took root in her chest and made it hard to breathe.

Things had been such a struggle back then. Her dad had been about as low on the ladder in the Army as you could get. Her mom got pregnant at seventeen. The only thing either of them seemed to do well was lose their temper. He was always gone on one long deployment or another, and then one time, he just never came back.

Finally, when she was about ten, CPS put an end to the cycle of poor choices her parents kept making. She lived with her grandmother for a few years, and then she met Trudy. Her dad's mother's sister didn't have any children of her own, but she had lots of love in her heart—and when Meg's caseworker searched for a relative to take responsibility, Trudy stepped up to the plate.

A seagull flew overhead, riding the unseen currents of the wind. Meg decided the bird's aimlessness was the perfect metaphor for what her life would have been without Trudy.

Socially, things hadn't been easy in Port Provident for an outsider with a sketchy background. But inside the walls of Trudy's small historic Victorian-era home, there had at least been love and good, solid life advice.

Most of that advice in her later high school years centered around staying away from Dan Clark.

Trudy wasn't convinced that the brash superstar could really have been in love with her great-niece. She sensed something wasn't what it seemed at the time.

When Dan gave her up so easily in a trade for glory on the field, Meg knew Trudy had been right.

But without learning that lesson the hard way, Meg wouldn't have Ellie in her life.

And Ellie made all the whispers at bus stops, tears on her pillow, and struggles to find herself worth it.

But now...she had returned to Port Provident and had to confront not only her past with Dan, but the future with their daughter.

And Meg just didn't want to do it.

"I'd like the biggest coffee you have, in the strongest form you have it," she said simply to the barista behind the counter.

"We have a new Caribbean blue free trade. Would you like to try that? We just got it in Monday and everyone is raving about it."

Meg nodded. "As long as it packs a punch, I'll take it. And if it could magically transport me to the Caribbean, that would be good too."

The barista laughed. "Well, it can't do that, but maybe you could go down to the marina and get yourself a charter."

"Now there's an idea. Maybe I could."

The barista rung up Meg's purchase. "Gretel's Great Escapes does boat tours for tourists."

"I'm not really a tourist," Meg said, handing the barista her card to swipe for payment. She wasn't really a resident either. Just one more way she didn't fit in Port Provident. She couldn't wait for Trudy's physical therapy to be done so Meg and Ellie could head back to Austin. Life in a large city where she could be completely anonymous suited her. Something was always going on in Austin. The citizens there occupied themselves with things other than gossip and speculation about Meg and her life. Everyone in Austin seemed to come from somewhere and have some kind of quirk. It made them less likely to care about hers.

But not in Port Provident.

Being all up in your neighbor's business was just part of living in a small town.

And Meg hated every single bit of it.

"Gretel's over at Pier 31. You should go see what the schedule today is."

Meg signed the receipt and handed it back across the counter. "Wait. Did you say Gretel? As in Gretel Conway? There can't be that many Gretels in Port Provident, right?"

"Nope. She's the one and only." The barista handed the hot coffee to Meg. "Here you go."

Meg took the beverage and took a deep breath of the richly scented steam rising off it. Gretel Conway had been one of her first friends in Port Provident. In high school, they'd been part of the business club together. But after Meg moved to Austin with Dan, they'd lost touch. "I think I will head over there. Thanks for the tip."

Pier 31 looked much like every other pier along Harborview Drive. A non-descript white booth at the beginning of an inclined walkway read "Harbor Tour Tickets" in blue letters. Nowhere did any of the signs say anything about Gretel or a great escape. Meg scanned the area and a shot of nervousness burst through her. She tried to dismiss it as the caffeine hitting her system, but clearly the barista had directed her incorrectly.

"Can I help you?" a voice from a white boat shouted toward Meg.

Ugh. Meg hated merely talking to strangers. Shouting back at them seemed like torture. "Um, I'm looking for Gretel's Great Escapes."

"Found it!" The person on the boat hopped over onto the dock. She had flame-colored hair, clearly dyed, and it stuck straight up in a short, spunky 'do. She hadn't advanced five steps up the walkway before realizing who her potential customer was. "I'm Gretel. Wait a minute. Meg? What are you doing here? Vacation?"

Meg waved. It felt good to have someone besides Trudy excited about her appearance in town. Dan's reaction in the field house was shock. And then at the elementary school, it was, well...whatever could be classified as stronger than shock. Not that she blamed him.

"No, I'm here to help Trudy with some catering jobs on her books while she recovers from knee surgery. She had a few things on her schedule that she didn't want to cancel, and her doctors weren't willing to put the operation off any longer."

Gretel reached out and embraced her old friend. "So how long are you here for?"

"Maybe a month or two? Maybe a little longer. It depends on how Trudy's physical therapy does. We'll definitely be gone by Christmas."

"We? So, you're married again?"

Meg's heart took on water and sank a little bit. She wasn't used to biting her tongue. In Austin, no one knew Dan anymore—no one cared about a washed-up quarterback. But here, everyone knew Dan. He was practically royalty back in his hometown. And so, that meant no one on this island except Trudy had ever heard of Ellie.

But with this morning's revelation, all that secrecy became unnecessary.

Meg wondered what it would be like to live in truth here where she spent most of her formative years. No more secrets.

"I have a daughter, Ellie."

"You do? That's awesome. I've got a daughter too. Hattie's eight. How old is Ellie?"

Meg swallowed hard. She knew as soon as she answered, Gretel would likely do the math.

But...truth.

"She's almost nine-and-a-half."

"Really? How cool that they're almost the same age...hey, then, um..."

Bingo. Meg could read the thought as it flashed across Gretel's mind.

"So, is she... Wait. Dan's never mentioned having a daughter." Gretel's brow furrowed slightly.

Meg looked at the glints of sun on the bobbing water in the harbor. They just kept shining, no matter what the current below did. She wished it was that easy.

But maybe it actually was.

"She is." Meg pushed out the simple words before she could take them back. "Dan hasn't been involved in her life."

Meg felt relief at owning the truth of Ellie's parentage. But almost instantly, that small feeling of victory got pushed aside. She hadn't owned the full sphere of the truth.

"He...um... he didn't know. Circumstances were complicated before Ellie was born. I've raised her as a single mother."

Gretel plucked her sunglasses off her head. "The single mom gig is a tough one, isn't it? I've been doing it for years myself. Sometimes, things just work out that way. But we're all on our own path for a reason, and I've learned to just honor that and keep moving forward."

The straightforward wisdom in Gretel's words made Meg smile shyly. Gretel didn't judge. Instead, she got it. All of a sudden, Meg didn't feel quite so alone. She felt stronger than she had in years. Ten years, to be specific.

"I think you're right, Gretel. I really do."

"So, did you come for a boat ride? We're about to do a harbor dolphin tour. There's one family on board, but that's it. So, maybe you and I could catch up while my captain, Esteban, does the navigating."

Meg looked at the light on the water again. It called to her, telling her to go be a part of something spontaneous for a change. She was tired of hiding, tired of bearing a burden. Open water and an old friend might be just the ticket to freedom she was looking for today.

DAN LOVED THE LIGHTS on the football field. Friday Night Lights were *a thing* in Texas: a legend, a mystique. High school football was as much a part of the culture here as barbeque and cowboys. And for twenty or so years, the minute the lights flipped on, Dan had always known it was his time to step up and shine.

Whether it was as a player, or now as a coach, Dan loved the spotlight and the crowd and the chance to be his best.

But never had the bulbs overhead burned brighter than tonight. And for the first time, it all terrified him.

He'd left two tickets at will call. One for Meg, and one for their daughter.

Meg had seen him play on this very field before, but Ellie never had. Did she even know why she was coming tonight? Would she be embarrassed that her dad had washed out of playing football and now walked around the sidelines with a clipboard because he couldn't give up the game he loved?

Would she think he put football before her?

It scared him to realize that was an honest assessment. He didn't know about her then, but he knew himself, and he knew Meg had been right. In the days before Ellie had been born, Dan's eyes were set on glory—NFL glory—and nothing, not even a child on the way, would have dissuaded him from his goal. His young marriage, young wife, and young child were casualties to his dreams.

The keyword was young.

Young Dan had been cocky and self-assured.

Young Dan had allowed the wrong voices to speak in his ear.

Young Dan had been wrong.

Now, he'd been back at Port Provident High School for five years, and the school board named their one-time high school hero as head coach two seasons ago. He'd had the chance to invest in the lives of these kids, and that had been greater than any victory he'd won on any field.

But he hadn't had the chance to invest in his own kid.

He cursed under his breath at the futility of the choices he'd made and the current situation they'd led to.

Dan scanned the crowd. The tickets were all general admission, so he had no way of knowing where Meg would choose to sit. But he knew she'd be here. She'd given her word.

My word's all I have Dan…I don't have anything else to give you. So, when I say I'll marry you and follow you anywhere, I mean it.

Meg's words at the edge of this very field before the homecoming game their senior year of high school flooded back as a reminder. He could still feel the buzz of energy. College coaches were there to see his game in person that night. It was a night he knew everything could change for him. He'd pulled Meg off to the side before the game for a quick kiss and he couldn't bring himself to leave her side until he knew she was coming with him, no matter which of those colleges offered him a scholarship and a path to see his dreams come true.

It had all been crazy. He'd been crazy. Crazy in love with the shy, brown-haired girl who'd captured his heart when she'd started making sure his math grades stayed up. He'd been crazy enough to believe all his dreams would come true—Meg and football and everything else.

Although just about everything had changed since that kiss, he doubted Meg's commitment to her word had changed. After all, she'd given it to Barry and walked away to be a single mom because she believed that's what Dan wanted.

He knew she'd be here.

He just needed to find where she sat in the crowd.

Maybe then his pulse would quit racing. Maybe then he could focus on the game. His kids on the field needed him.

But so did his kid in the stands.

This would be his biggest night ever, and it wouldn't have a thing to do with football.

About halftime, Dan picked Meg out in the stands. Once the band left to come down on the field, it made it easier to scan the stands.

"Can you tell me what the problem is, man?" Zack came and stood by Dan after substituting a player on the field. "Bowman just ran that play all kinds of wrong and you forgot to give him the chewing out he deserves. I don't know where your head is, but it's not in this game."

Dan pointed across the green field. "Over there."

Zack let out a low whistle. "She came to the game?"

"I asked her," Dan said matter-of-factly. He tucked his clipboard against his chest with one folded arm and pretended to watch the snap in front of him. "She said she'd come. She did."

"Whoa. Wait a minute. She's not alone. I thought Lamont Brown was the only kid Trudy Malvern was fostering right now."

Dan nodded. "He is."

"So...who's the kid she's sharing popcorn with?"

"Her name's Ellie. Ellie Clark."

Zack dropped the water bottle he'd been holding. "Ellie Clark? You're kidding me, right, man?"

"No, I'm not."

"You have a kid? She hid your kid from you?"

Zack's volume began to raise. Even with all the commotion on the sidelines and on the field, it wouldn't have been hard for anyone nearby to get more than an earful.

"*Sssh*. Keep it down, Zack. She had her reasons."

"Horse poop." Zach spit out his frustration but lowered his voice. "There's no reason to keep a man's child from him. None. That's low."

"Have you seen Barry Haynes lately?"

Zach turned and faced Dan straight on. "You're just going to change the subject on me now?"

"Yup." Dan waved some signals with his hands to Chris Callison, the quarterback for the Port Provident Pirates. "So, have you? I heard Lamont had his number."

"Yeah, he's putting on a footwork drills camp on the mainland over the fall break. A couple of the kids are going. He is going to do some film the kids can use in their recruiting videos."

"Nice work, Chris! There ya go!" Dan clapped as Chris' ball found the sweet spot right in the wide receiver's hands. Then he turned back to his best friend. "Cut the ties. None of these guys are going. None of them. Barry Haynes is not welcome around my program or my players."

"What are you talking about, Dan? Barry Haynes has a lot of connections. We can't alienate him. Look at most of these kids. Football is their ticket out. It's how they're going to pay for their education."

Fire rose up in Dan. It hadn't been that long ago that he'd thought of football as the only way out for his own life, too. And most of that belief had been stoked by Barry Haynes. Back then, he believed in Barry almost more than he believed in himself.

And instead of bringing him everything, it had cost him everything. Barry knew about Ellie and didn't tell Dan. He never wanted to see Barry Haynes again. He'd let Zack take care of the conversation cutting him off from the program. Dan didn't trust himself to control his anger if he came face-to-face with Barry ever again.

All that anger abated, though, when he looked across the field.

Ellie dug in the bucket of popcorn and grabbed out a huge handful, then grinned at her mother.

Dan looked up at the sky so he wouldn't be overwhelmed by the emotion of seeing pure joy on his daughter's face for the first time. He'd missed all the Christmases, all the birthday parties, all the smiles...all the love.

God, she's beautiful. You did good in making her. I just want to know her. I just want the chance.

He looked back at Zack and set his jaw. "Barry Haynes doesn't come near my program ever again. Tell the coaches. Tell the guys. There are other ways for these kids to succeed...without Barry."

PIRATE STADIUM WASN'T oversized or flashy like so many Texas high school football stadiums had become these days. There were stadiums in the suburbs of Austin and Dallas that had nine-figure price tags. High school football had become big business. In that respect, Barry Haynes had been ahead of the curve when he took Dan Clark under his wing after he started on Port Provident's varsity team as a sophomore.

The stadium had been spruced up in the years that Meg had been gone, but the underlying bones still held the same echoes. This place felt familiar.

At one point in her life, she'd have said it felt like home.

She'd felt like a queen for the first time in her life here. Right over there, to be specific. Meg turned her head to the left and looked at the tunnel leading to the locker room. About five steps away from there, she'd been hanging over the rail from the bleachers, cheering for Dan as he jogged off the field from a victory. He ran over to the wall and jumped up, grabbing her hand.

"Come here," he said, and pulled her over the rail. His arms caught her with all the accuracy he showed throwing a ball. "You're my good luck charm. We weren't supposed to beat these guys."

She felt the prickly turf scratching at the soles of her flip flops. It crunched under her feet as Dan pulled her close. Teammates ran by him, slapping at his shoulder pads and the seat of his pants. He never took his eyes off her.

He put a hand behind her head, cupping the curve of her skull gently, then he leaned close. "Can I kiss you, Lady Luck?"

She breathed in the air and knew she'd remember the scent of popcorn and nacho cheese for the rest of her life. She didn't want to speak, didn't want anyone else except Dan to hear what was in her heart. "Mmhmm," she said.

Dan closed the distance between them, pressing his lips against hers. She knew several of their classmates were hollering around them, but Meg heard nothing but the sound of the blood rushing in her ears from her head to her heart to her toes and back again.

She'd never been kissed before. It felt like everything the magazines and TV shows made it out to be.

With nothing but instinct—and a few things she'd read in teen magazines—to guide her, she ran one fingertip up the arm he held his helmet with. Softly, he teased the canyon between her lips with his tongue. Meg gasped, and Dan pulled back.

His hand dropped from her hair back to his side, but his smile lingered. "You'll be here next Friday, won't you?"

"Of course I will," she said. Her head swam, drunk on heady emotion and teenage hormones.

"Good. I like having you around. I'd like you to stay around. I'd like you to be my girlfriend."

Meg matched his smile with her own. Prince Charming wasn't supposed to choose the nerd who loved math and who wasn't popular. Cinderella only got her happily ever after in fairy tales. But here was Dan Clark, kissing her for everyone to see. She reached out her hand and took his, then squeezed. She wanted to hold on to the moment forever.

Forever didn't last.

But at least Pirate Stadium had. The crowd around her cheered as the home team scored yet another victory. She had to admit it, Dan was a good coach. The talent between the Pirates and the other team seemed pretty even, but the Port Provident play-calling kept their opponents on their toes. The Pirates even ran a wildcat play to close out the third quarter, which got the fans on their feet. Ellie tossed popcorn in the air to celebrate a sneaky run across the goal line.

It surprised Meg to realize she was in the same place with Dan Clark, watching his football team on the field, and she was having fun.

But that had nothing to do with Dan, she knew. It had everything to do with Ellie.

Ellie was the light in her life and seeing her enjoy the game took Meg's mind off what surely had to come.

After the clock ran out and the school fight song had been sung by victorious Port Provident fans and players alike, Dan came into Meg's line of sight. Two more steps would bring him to where they'd both stood twelve years before. He looked down at the turf, then stopped and turned around.

Meg could tell he knew exactly where his feet were placed. And it wasn't hard to see that the same thoughts which formed in her mind earlier were now running full speed through his.

Dan looked up in the stands, and locked eyes with her almost immediately.

She knew his eyes were topaz. She knew they seemed as studious as a cat crossing the Serengeti something was on his mind. And even across this stadium—across all the years—she still knew *him*.

It hit her right in the part of her heart she'd sworn had been closed up like a medieval dungeon. She'd put chains and bars and locks on it the moment Barry handed her that letter and asked her to be out of the apartment by the end of the weekend. Surprise overtook Meg. She didn't think she'd ever see Dan again, much less feel something when she did.

But here she stood, surrounded by a crowd in Pirate Stadium where, basically, it all began.

Dan raised one eyebrow and tilted his head slightly left. Meg knew he was indicating Ellie's presence. He was asking her permission to meet his child.

Meg didn't plan on this day ever coming. Ellie asked about her dad once, back at parent night in Kindergarten, but had never asked again—and Meg never pushed it.

Tonight, though, that all changed. Meg couldn't stop the speeding train headed her way. She felt a quiver in her arms, a shaking in the pit of the stomach. The inevitable scared her.

Then, she remembered something Gretel's words from yesterday. *Honor it and keep moving forward.* Something in that small corner of her heart told her not to fight what flew toward the horizon.

Meg nodded her head and raised her hand, curling her fingers once, then twice, letting Dan know it was okay to come.

She leaned over slightly toward Ellie, then pointed across the field. "Punkin', there's someone I'd like for you to meet."

DAN STOPPED AT A GATE in wall separating the seating from the field.

His mouth had gotten more and more dry with every step across the turf. He didn't know how it would form words and speak. He knew he should have been watching Ellie as she walked down the steps between the bleachers, but instead, he couldn't keep his eyes off Meg.

What would she say?

Pirate Stadium was one of the most familiar places in his life. Yet everything right here, right now, seemed so surreal.

"Hey Coach! Great game!" A group of parents waved and clapped as they walked past. Usually, Dan enjoyed taking the time to dissect victories with Pirate fans, but not tonight. All he could do right now was acknowledge them with a half-wave. They passed by, and then there was nothing between Dan and the family he never knew he had.

"Dan, this is Ellie." Meg placed a hand on the little girl's back, gently steering her toward the gate.

He reached out his hand to shake it in introduction. Ellie gave him a trusting smile and reached her hand back toward him. She looked beautiful. In a few years, she'd be stunning. She had his eyes and height and coloring paired with the roundness of Meg's cheeks and smile.

She wore the same friendly expression her mother used to wear. The same expression that made him fall in love with Meg once upon a time now made him fall immediately in love with the legacy they'd created together.

He hadn't known any feeling could be this thorough. Dan had never even spoken a word to Eleanor Danielle Clark, and yet, he knew he'd love her forever.

Dan took Ellie's hand and closed his fingers around hers. He'd held the hands of so many kids throughout the years. But never his own flesh and blood.

"It's nice to meet you, Ellie." Dan knew himself to be a liar as he told her that simple sentence. It was so much more than nice to meet her, but he didn't know how to put his shock and elation into the right words.

He looked up at Meg. She bit her lower lip. This wasn't easy for either of them. And when Ellie found out who he really was, how would she react?

"So, do you know my mom from high school?" Ellie asked.

Dan nodded. "I do. She was a good friend."

Back then, she'd been the best friend he had. Everyone else expected something from him because of his talent and his position within the hierarchy of the school. But not Meg. She just laughed at his bad jokes and helped him with his trigonometry homework and brought bags of sour cream and onion potato chips to every practice so he'd have his favorite snack.

"Ell, Dan was actually my boyfriend in high school."

Ellie looked at her mom and laughed. "You kissed the football coach?"

Meg tossed her head back and laughed, a sound Dan hadn't realized he'd missed until just now. "More than once, actually. In fact, remember how I told you a few years ago that I got married really young and it didn't work out?"

"Yeah..." Ellie's voice turned skeptical.

A knot formed in Dan's stomach as the moment of truth bore down on their small trio.

"Well, that's him." The left corner of Meg's mouth twisted down while her right eyebrow quirked up.

"Huh. Cool. I guess." Ellie put her hands on her hips. "So, like you could have been my dad or something."

"Actually, Punkin', he *is* your dad." Meg's tone was gentle but no-nonsense.

Ellie looked right at Dan. He quickly decided that smiling was probably the best route. If she could sense the intensity of the emotions in his body at this moment, she'd take off running up the stairs, screaming at the top of her lungs.

"Wait a second. Is that why we came back to Port Provident? Are we moving here for good or something?"

Meg shook her head. "No, we came because Trudy needed us. We're going back to Austin when she's well. But if you want to get to know your dad while you're here, that's okay."

"And if you don't want to, I mean, that's okay too. I know this is probably surprising for you." Dan thought he should throw it out there. He wanted to know his daughter, but Meg had made it clear that it would be Ellie's choice. He wanted them to know he respected that.

"No, I mean, that's cool. I've never had a dad before."

Dan didn't even know he'd been holding his breath. But suddenly, a flood of oxygen hit his brain.

Ellie declared the situation to be "cool."

His daughter wanted to get to know him.

Dan knew all about Xs and Os and game plans. He felt more confident about those two letters than the other twenty-four combined. He could do this. He just needed a game plan.

Ellie would be going back to her regular life soon. But in the meantime, he had a few weeks to get to know her. And, if he could atone for a stupid letter that once-upon-a-time he was too much of a coward to deliver himself, he would do that too.

Chapter Four

SATURDAYS IN THE FALL were made for two things. Watching college football and walking along the beach. The tourists had all gone back to their regular homes and routines. The beaches were largely deserted and the weather held a touch of impending milder weather.

Dan breathed in deeply and looked out at the water. He felt content.

He didn't know what would come next between him and Meg and Ellie. But he knew Meg—well, *had known* Meg—and there was no doubt that she'd do what was right for Ellie. Whether or not he was able to carve out a place in Ellie's life, his daughter would be okay.

She'd grown up with love and with her mother's laughter. Meg didn't have those in her own early childhood, so Dan knew his ex-wife would have made those a priority for her own child. For that, Dan felt nothing but gratitude.

He had a daughter—it still felt surreal to say the words to himself—and she was growing up beautifully, both inside and out.

Dan's mother had a framed Bible verse hanging in the study of his childhood home and a snippet of it came to his mind as he looked at the waves. "Her children arise and call her blessed," the Proverb above Mary Ellen Clark's desk said.

He'd always thought of that verse in relation to his mother. Proverbs thirty-one catalogued the attributes of a righteous woman, and as a child, he'd thought Mary Ellen possessed them all.

But now, the verse took on new meaning. It applied to Meg too. Dan remembered the smile on Ellie's face as she shared popcorn and laughter with her mother in the stands of the football game. He reflected on the spirited wave in the Port Provident Elementary hallway.

Without a doubt, Meg was blessed.

And he'd been the fool who let her go.

What did that make him?

"Hey, um, Dad..." The voice behind him sounded sweet as a cupful of sugar, even as it hesitated slightly.

"Ellie! Hey!" Dan immediately chastised himself. *Settle down. Don't scare her off. Play it cool.*

Dan saw Meg a few steps away, locking her car. She'd parked in one of the parallel spaces along Gulfview Boulevard. The wind blew a few tendrils of hair out of the messy bun she'd wound near the crown of her head.

Surely ten years hadn't passed. He knew he'd changed a lot in that time, but Meg hadn't.

"We brought donuts. Mom said she used to dream about Starfish Donuts." Ellie brought a white paper sack over to Dan. She held it out, then angled shyly towards him. It was more of a lean than a hug, but he'd take it. It was a good start to their first family day.

Dan slipped his hand around Ellie's shoulder and gave it a squeeze.

He closed his eyes for just a flicker of a second, wanting to imprint in his mind forever the memory of his first hug with his only child.

"Starfish makes the best donuts. They're definitely worthy of dreams. I bring them for the guys on Friday mornings."

"I bet you have to bring a lot of them. I guess football players can eat a ton of donuts, huh?" Ellie reached in the bag and grabbed a glazed donut hole.

"They can. Luckily, Barbara at Starfish knows I'm coming every Friday and makes extra for me. What's your favorite donut, Ellie?"

It seemed important to know. He had so much little trivia like this to catch up on.

"The regular donuts with the chocolate on top." She swallowed the rest of the donut hole in record time.

"Chocolate frosted. Duly noted."

Ellie licked a finger. "What's yours?"

"The same."

"So, we've got donuts in common." She beamed a smile in his direction.

"It seems that we do."

Meg's flip-flops scattered sand as she walked toward them. "Did you save me any, Ellie?"

Ellie scrunched her face before exaggeratedly searching the small bag. "Dad just said he likes chocolate frosted, just like I do. So, this one is his. There's a bunch of donut holes left."

"Donut holes, huh? I see where Mom ranks now." She laughed as Ellie handed chocolate-covered goodness to Dan and two tiny spheres to Meg.

Meg had turned it into a joke, but Dan wondered if there was some truth in her sentiment. Did she worry that she'd be replaced? That Ellie would see the new presence of her dad like a shiny toy at Christmas—the hot new thing?

He didn't want to replace Meg in Ellie's life.

He knew he *couldn't* replace Meg in Ellie's life.

But Ellie was only nine. She wouldn't know all that.

Dan tore the donut down the middle. "Let's share."

He gave the peace offering to Meg and looked steadily in her gray eyes. She met his gaze and didn't even blink. She gave him a half-smile.

"Maybe so. Let's see if we can work something out." She took the donut from his hand and then took a bite.

She'd given him a gift. The gift of just a chance...the hope of a chance. He would take it, and do so with a grateful heart.

"Have you ever been to the beach before, Ellie?"

"Nope. My friend Lily has a boat and we get to go out on Lady Bird Lake in Austin sometimes though. Her dad's teaching me to waterski."

Everything he had lost jumped up and knocked Dan emotionally flat, as though he'd just been hit by a rogue wave. Someone else was taking his daughter out on a boat. Someone else was taking her to waterski.

Dan crossed his arms and swallowed hard. The words he wanted to say got caught in his throat. All he could put together was a short prayer, running like lightning through his brain.

I can't mess this up, God.

But what, exactly, was "this"? What path was he asking for God's assistance in making straight? His path with Ellie? Yes, definitely.

Dan looked at Meg. The early sunlight stole through the thin fuzz of clouds above and teased out red highlights in her hair.

There's another path, God. Is it too much for me to hope we can straighten it out, too?

Ellie took off running toward where the last rolls of the surf spread out to caress the sand of Port Provident's beaches. Her laughter carried on the wind.

Meg watched their daughter take in the thrill of her first trip to the coast, completely unaware that Dan watched Meg with equal fascination. From the outside, she hadn't changed since the first day she sat next to him in a high school trigonometry class and asked if she could borrow a pencil.

He knew his actions had changed her from the inside, though.

And now he knew, beyond any doubt, that the choices he'd made changed him too. One thing hadn't changed, though. It took this moment, back on the beach with Meg—watching the daughter they now shared together—to know that all the years, all the choices, all the secrets, all the regret...none of it changed one thing.

Nothing changed the fact that he was still in love with Meg McMahon.

He'd spent a lifetime focused on winning. Now, he would not stop until he'd won her back, body and soul.

AT LEAST ONE FRONT row parking spot remained. Meg had worried that the parking situation on Saturday night at Porter's Seafood would resemble a madhouse. As the oldest family-owned seafood restaurant in continuous operation on the Texas Gulf Coast, Porter's was legendary. Visitors to Port Provident and residents alike made time in their busy schedules to stop and eat a succulent meal while watching the sun set over the waves. It was a time-honored tradition.

Misgiving after misgiving crowded Meg's heart and mind about meeting Dan for dinner. So at least getting a good parking spot meant one thing tonight would go right, even if nothing else did.

Meg's first instinct had been to decline the invitation. But Ellie had overheard Dan's request and informed her mother that she needed to go.

So, reluctantly, Meg said yes—on one condition. She told Dan she'd meet him at Porter's. Allowing him to pick her up at Trudy's felt too much like a date.

The past needed to remain in the past.

She walked through the doors. It felt like a time warp. Dan had taken her to Porter's for dinner the night he proposed. Meg hadn't been back since.

How could she have forgotten?

Hard work, that's how. She'd worked hard to move on with her life and create something she was proud of. Besides raising Ellie, Meg took Barry's education fund, left Lone Star University behind, and attended culinary school. Afterwards, she'd risen to the level of executive chef at one of Austin's best boutique hotels until they completed a merger with a national chain a few weeks ago.

She'd built a new life, brick by brick. It took years of hard work and a litany of reminders to never look back.

Walking through the door of Porter's felt like a tug on a thread that could unravel it all.

"Meg!" Dan smiled and waved from where he'd been talking with a small group of people waiting on a table. He gave one of the men a handshake and a pat on the back as he disengaged from the conversation and made his way across the waiting area.

As he came up to Meg, he started to lean forward, then stopped himself.

She stiffened, then relaxed slightly as she realized she would not be wrapped in the hug that seemed to be coming. Thankfully, whatever Dan had been thinking, he'd thought better of it. This wasn't a date. This was a co-parenting discussion between two people who shared a child. Ellie deserved their best effort and cooperation.

Meg could do anything, as long as it was for Ellie.

She could sit across from the man who had once held her heart and proposed to her after a meal right under this very roof. She would do it for Ellie.

"Thanks for coming tonight. I thought it would be good if we could talk without Ellie for a little bit. She's a great kid—but there are some grown-up type conversations it seems like we need to have."

Meg nodded in agreement. "We do. And she *is* a great kid. But it's probably better if we do this on our own and then present a united front to her."

"I agree."

"Coach Clark? We've got your table ready." The hostess pointed toward the main dining room. "Follow me, please."

The waiting area was crowded with a multi-hour wait of people willing to stand in line for a table. But it seemed as though every one of them knew Dan Clark. There were multiple shouts of his name and more than one high-five, congratulating him on last night's victory.

Dan Clark was still the king of Port Provident.

Meg tried to keep a smile on her face as she walked beside him, but a question stirred in her mind. If Dan was still the golden son of this small island, what did that make her?

She was still searching for an answer as the hostess stopped by a table in an alcove. It faced the expanse of windows that showed the majesty of the ocean just across Gulfview Boulevard.

It was the table she'd last sat at with Dan the night he proposed.

Adrenaline slicked through her veins, pulsing thick and sticky like worn motor oil. If Meg looked at the table, she remembered that night. If she closed her eyes, she remembered that night. Her head became as light as if she'd started sucking on a helium balloon. Port Provident was filled with nothing but memories—and the island's once and future king—and she couldn't get away from any of them.

She wanted to be able to do anything for Ellie. But sitting at this table...this she couldn't do.

"Meg?" Dan reached out and took her hand with one of his own. He braced her back with the other. "Are you okay? What's the matter?"

His quick glance tore between her face and the table and the view beyond.

"Oh, Sheryl," he said to the hostess. "Hey, we're gonna need another table."

The teenager picked up the menus from where she'd just laid them on the table. "Okay, Coach. Um, which one would you like?"

Dan's eyes connected with Meg's, questioning. Meg shook her head. She felt a hot wave of embarrassment at not being able to control her reaction.

"How about that one back there?" Dan pointed to a small round table on the far edge of the room. It still had a view of the water, but nothing else about it drew any similarities to past history.

"Okay. Mr. Porter asked me to put you at one of the window tables. Are you sure?"

He squeezed Meg's hands once, twice. His grip was strong, but in a reassuring way.

"Completely."

They followed Sheryl to the smaller table in the corner. "Thank you," Meg said softly as the hostess lit the candle in the middle of their new location.

Dan pulled out the chair for Meg, then scooted her gently to the edge of the table. He hadn't put a foot wrong since she walked in the door of Porter's. Clearly, she was the only one suffering with the past and insecurities. Meg held up her menu, hoping it would block her face at least partially while she tried to rearrange her features and get a grip on her emotions.

She didn't want to admit it, but maybe if she just accepted the one obvious fact, she could find some way to achieve her ultimate goal. The only thing that mattered was moving forward for Ellie.

But the indisputable fact had become perfectly clear. Dan Clark still affected Meg McMahon.

HE SHOULD HAVE SUGGESTED anywhere but Porter's.

Dan hadn't been trying to send some kind of subliminal message. While he'd eaten at Porter's probably two hundred times since the night he proposed, clearly, Meg had not.

"I really just wanted us to be able to talk. I didn't mean to bring up the past."

She took a sip of water before replying. "This island is small, Dan. Everywhere is the past. We aren't going to be able to escape it. It's fine. I feel like I overreacted."

"No, I completely understand." Dan took a slice of crusty French bread out of the basket between them. "But maybe...maybe we don't need to escape the past. Without the past, there wouldn't be an Ellie, you know?"

He saw Meg's shoulders straighten from the slumped position they'd shifted to as soon as he Meg greeted her at the hostess stand.

"She's been everything to me, Dan. You're very right. No matter what, I have no regrets."

"I do." Dan placed the bread back on the small plate to his left. "I missed out on life with my daughter. I missed out on life with my wife. I missed out on my family. Meg, I can't use words to make up for any of the time I've lost or the things I did to cause the breakdown in our marriage. But I can ask your forgiveness."

He laid his hands on the table in front of him, palms up.

"These hands are as empty as my life has been. I didn't know it until you came back to town, but there's no way to deny that I know it now."

Meg didn't reply.

Dan didn't know what he'd been expecting in return for baring his soul, but it wasn't silence. Unfortunately, he had no choice but to accept her response—even if it was no response at all.

The tablecloth stirred ever so slightly. Meg laid a balled-up cloth napkin near her bread plate.

She placed one hand atop Dan's left hand, and then gently rested her other hand atop his right.

The earth didn't shake. The clouds didn't break. Time didn't shift.

But everything fell into place with her touch.

"Let's move forward. For Ellie. Even for us." She inhaled slowly and exhaled deliberately. "I think...I think we both deserve it, Dan."

Dan swallowed past the lump in his throat. "How do you want to move forward, Meg?"

"I want you to spend time with Ellie. I want you to get to know her. I want her to have a dad. I know the football season is busy for you, but maybe in the spring we could work out a visitation schedule?"

He let out a long breath of his own. "I'd like that. If you want to get lawyers involved to make it official, I understand."

"I'd prefer if we could just do this together. I lost my job a few weeks ago. I don't have extra money for legal fees right now."

"We can do that. We're both adults and we both want what's best for Ellie."

She smiled, and everything she'd said about moving forward got swept away in a memory of the past. In his mind's eye, he saw eighteen-year-old Meg sitting at that table across that room in a yellow strapless sundress, beaming from ear-to-ear.

He'd loved her so much then.

The honesty between them tonight broke down the barrier that had popped up when he saw her in the field house at the beginning of the week. Actually, it broke down the barrier that had stood since the day he made the biggest mistake of his life and believed Barry Haynes instead of his own heart.

Before either of them realized it, their plates were cleared and dinner was over.

"You want dessert, don't you?" Dan winked across the table at Meg.

She laughed. "I'm that easy to read, huh?"

"You've never been able to say no to cheesecake. I figure some things just don't change."

"You'd be right. And the worst part is, Ellie's an enabler. There's not a lot of willpower in our house when it comes to dessert."

Dan waved their waiter over and put in an order for Meg. Once it arrived, Meg wasted no time in swirling the cream cheese pie with the strawberry puree poured over the top. It made Dan happy to be able to make her smile—even if it was really the cheesecake bringing the joy.

"Is the lighthouse still there?" She popped another bite in her mouth.

"Yeah. They even repainted it after Hurricane Hope came through. It looks good. You wouldn't recognize the old gal."

"I loved to go there in the summers and read a book. The tourists never seemed to make it quite that far down the island."

Dan agreed. "It's a special place, that's for sure."

The Port Provident Lighthouse was special for a number of reasons, but there was no way Dan would bring up most of them. The evening was cruising along like a sports car on the open highway. He didn't want to put on the brakes.

Meg scraped the last little bit of strawberry sauce off the plate. "Will you take me there?"

"Tonight?"

She nodded. "I want to see the sunset from the lighthouse. I've missed it."

"I'll get the check." Dan was determined to soak up what time with Meg that he could while she was here helping Trudy. He would have taken her to the end of the world. All she had to do was ask.

Chapter Five

A BREEZE WITH A HINT of early fall crispness crossed the tip of Provident Island as Dan held the car door open for Meg. She could hear the low roar of the waves as they curled and rolled to shore below Point Provident, the higher outcrop where the lighthouse stood.

She stepped around the door and Dan closed it behind her. Meg hesitated slightly as she looked at the red-and-white striped beacon.

"Looks good, doesn't she?" Dan came behind Meg, blocking the tiny chill in the night air from settling on her shoulders.

"They did a good job fixing her up. You were right. The whole park looks so nice." Meg gave a half-laugh. "The tourists might find this place now."

This time, it was Dan's turn to laugh, and he did so—loudly. "Think of all the teenagers who will be disappointed to have their hiding place discovered. Where will they go to do...teenager things...now?"

"Teenager things. Ha. That's one way of putting it, Dan."

"I can think of about twenty different kinds of teenager things I tried here myself," he said, walking the edge of the point. Then he turned around and looked back at Meg. "And every one of them was with you."

"I remember." And she did. Her heart remembered, too. It began to beat faster and started to skip every third or fourth beat. Meg closed her eyes, feeling the spray of an errant wave that slapped the point a little too hard.

"So do I. You were the best friend I've ever had, Meg." He stood between her and the edge—in more ways than one. "You did more than save my grade in trig and my eligibility to keep playing. You saved *me*. No matter what, I'm a better person because of having you in my life. I mean it."

Meg knew the moon acted like a magnet on the coastal tides. She hadn't realized the pull affected her too, but without realizing it, she took two steps toward Dan. The gap between them was whisper-thin—and suddenly, the gap in time that they'd spent apart was no more than a breath as well.

Dan had earlier asked for forgiveness, and her words then had affirmed the request. They'd been able to laugh and enjoy dinner and plan for Ellie's future.

But forgiveness wasn't just words. Trudy had always told her forgiveness was a choice. Choices were decisions. And decisions came to life through actions.

One step closer to Dan. One action.

Another step. Another action.

"Meg."

She could see Dan swallow hard. Her own mouth had gone dry, leaving a tingle behind on her lips. She nodded in acknowledgement.

Dan lifted a hand and brushed back the hair blowing around Meg's face. He stroked a ribbon of hair between his thumb and forefinger, sliding the strands across his skin like an inspection of the finest silk. He looked up from and locked his gaze with Meg's.

The undertow in his brown-highlighted eyes pulled her beneath a wave of emotion like nothing she'd ever felt in her life, not even the first time she'd been to the lighthouse with Dan years ago.

"Meg," he said again. No one had said her name like that in forever. She knew the longing in her soul was also an action. It was an action that only Dan could complete. "Meg, I want to kiss you."

"I know."

She lifted her hand and smoothed it across his cheek, feeling the hint of roughness on his skin. She couldn't undo that action.

She didn't want to.

One more action—another step forward, this one the last literal part in the sequence of closing any gap between them.

Dan leaned his head down. Meg expected the kiss to be tentative, trying to bridge the years. But it wasn't.

This kiss meant to drink her in, to possess her. Her heart remembered. Her lips remembered. They recognized the other half that made them complete.

Her soul remembered. Oh, how it remembered.

A verse from Song of Solomon came into her head. *I have found the one who my soul loves.*

There was no use in denying to herself that she still loved Dan Clark. She'd always known it, but now she had no reason to deny it any longer. They shared a history. They shared a child. The two years of their marriage had been young, but it hadn't been a mistake. Only their divorce had. And now, she'd once again found the one she'd never stopped loving.

This time, her soul didn't want to let him go.

EVERY SUNDAY MORNING, Dan picked up a group of his football players and took them to church. So many of the young men he coached didn't have a strong father figure in their lives. Dan felt an obligation to stand in that gap.

But today was special. Today he wouldn't just be attending church with kids he served as a surrogate father to. Today, he would also be attending church with the one child he was a biological father to.

He and Meg stayed late at the lighthouse the night before, counting stars and talking about Ellie's future.

They even re-enacted one or two "teenage things" from their past. *Just like riding a bike*, Dan thought as the hint of a naughty smile crossed his face.

Meg asked about his team and his coaching, and when he invited her and Ellie to come along the next morning, she quickly accepted. He and the guys rotated between a few local churches so each young man could find a place where he felt he clicked. This morning, they were back at *La Iglesia de la Luz del Mundo*, a thriving congregation in the *La Missión* neighborhood of Port Provident.

"Guys, head on in and find a row where we can all sit together. Save two extra seats next to me, please, and one more for Lamont. He's coming too."

The teammates filed in. Dan stayed on the front steps, scanning the parking lot for Meg's tiny car. As it turned in to the parking lot and parked in a space on the back row, Dan realized he needed to wipe his hands on his pants. All of a sudden, his palms felt sweaty.

Ellie began to wave as soon as she saw him. Dan's heart leaped at the sight of his daughter. She took off running once she got to the sidewalk, and Dan picked her up in his arms and twirled her around in a tight bear hug. "Good morning, my sunshine," Dan said, as he gave her a kiss on the cheek.

He felt so much gratitude that Ellie had almost instantly accepted him, easily and fully. She'd embraced the idea of having a dad as readily as Dan had embraced knowing he had a daughter.

Meg smiled as she walked up.

Dan couldn't help himself. He leaned forward and his lips found her cheek.

"Good morning to you, too," Meg said. Ellie slid back toward the ground and Dan reached for Meg with his free hand.

"It is now. My two favorite ladies are here." Dan turned toward Lamont. "Hey, Lamont. The other guys are inside already."

"Okay, Coach. I'll find 'em." Lamont weaved through the crowd and shook Pastor Ruiz's hand as he walked in the door.

"I asked them to save us a few seats. It's okay with you if we sit by the team, right?"

"Of course it is. These are your kids. Coaching is who you are. I get it."

Dan shook his head. "It's who I was. I want to be someone different going forward. I want to be the husband and father I have a second chance to be. No more wasted chances, Meg."

Meg looked at him squarely. Her eyes were rounded and wide. Uh-oh. Maybe his honesty had been too much.

"Husband and father?"

"I don't want to scare you, Meg. But now I know what I lost, and I know what a gift it is to have another opportunity to get it right. I know I have to earn your trust, Meg." He stopped at the door to *La Iglesia*. He needed to get this out before they went inside. "I want to try. Can I have your permission to try, Meg?"

One second.

Two seconds.

Three seconds ticked by. Meg studied his face.

"Permission granted." She raised an eyebrow and smiled. "Don't let me down, Coach. Now, let's go to church."

AS THE AUTUMN WEEKS passed on Provident Island, Dan and Meg and Ellie fell into a comfortable routine. Football on Friday nights. Most Saturdays, Meg handled catering jobs for Trudy. Dan instituted Daddy-Daughter Date Days. And every Sunday morning, they'd take some of the Port Provident Pirates football team to church and lunch.

Dan leaned back in his chair in his office in the field house. He wanted to pat himself on the back.

His game plan was working.

Now, if he could just find a way to convince Meg to stay in Port Provident a little longer. Trudy's rehabilitation program seemed to be progressing and pretty soon, she'd be back to running her catering company without Meg's assistance.

And that would mean the end of time with his daughter and time with the love of his life.

A short knock sounded at the office door. "Got a sec?"

Zach Brumley stood in the doorway.

"Yeah, what's up?" Dan knew he should have moved his feet from off the top of his desk, but he was far too comfortable. He and Zach didn't stand on any kind of ceremony, anyway.

"Meg called."

Dan popped to attention and dropped his feet to the floor. The spring in his padded chair kicked everything up straight. "You talked to her? What did she say?"

Zach stifled a laugh. "You look like a high schooler with a crush. Obvious, much?"

"Well, the last time I had a crush on her, I *was* a high schooler. Does that count?"

"Not really. I'm just going to use this as an excuse to talk trash to you for a long time."

"Shut it." Dan leaned forward and tried to sound in control of the situation. He was pretty sure he was failing miserably. "What'd she say?"

"She forgot that she had a parent-teacher conference today to discuss how Ellie is transitioning at her new school. So she can't meet you at the lighthouse before practice." Zach leaned against the door jamb and raised an eyebrow. "The lighthouse, huh?"

Dan furrowed his own brow. "She likes watching the waves."

"I'm sure." Zach nodded his head deliberately. "I've taken a girl or two there myself. And I knew you at eighteen. So yeah, I know y'all are absolutely going there to check out high tide. But..."

Zach didn't finish his sentence. Dan decided to needle him a little bit. "But what? You don't think I could be as legendary at the lighthouse today as I was at eighteen?"

All of a sudden, a cloud crossed his best friend's face. "No, that wasn't it at all."

Dan couldn't figure out why Zach had gotten so serious. "Then what is it?"

"I don't know, man, but if it's a parent-teacher conference, and you're Ellie's parent, shouldn't you be there too? Or is she really not serious about all this co-parenting and family stuff you've been talking about since you put all that water between y'all under the bridge?"

He hadn't been given cause to doubt Meg—really, ever. But he couldn't shake the doubt that sprinted into his brain. Zach's words made sense.

"I'm sure she's got a good reason." Dan checked his watch. "Can you cover for me for a bit? I'd like to just run by the house and talk to her about it before she heads to the school."

Zach nodded. "Sure. I don't mean to make you freak out or anything..."

"You're not. It's just good to ask the questions and discuss instead of keeping everything bottled up. If I'd talked to Meg more in the first place, I wouldn't have spent the last decade in the dark about having a daughter."

"You're right. Get outta here. I'll cover for you."

Dan pulled up in front of Trudy's house. Meg's car wasn't out front, but maybe she'd parked in the driveway off the back alley. He took the stairs to the front porch two at a time, then knocked on the door.

It seemed like no one was home. Dan checked his watch again. He thought he'd made it in enough time. But maybe not. Dan made a mental note to just bring it up the next time he saw her. It would be too late for him to attend the parent-teacher conference by then, but he reminded himself that open lines of communication were the most important thing.

So why didn't Meg tell you?

Doubt danced in his mind with all the grace and presence of a hippopotamus in a tutu.

The doorknob rattled.

Good. He'd have his chance to talk with Meg after all. He could get the hippo off the main stage in his brain.

The door swung open, but instead of seeing Meg, Trudy stood there. She leaned heavily on a cane.

"She's not here, Dan. I'll tell her you stopped by." Trudy used her free hand to push the door back in place.

Dan put a hand around the edge of the door. "Trudy, wait."

"Dan, I'm tired. I'd like to just sit down."

He gestured to the swing on the front porch. "That's fine."

She scowled. "I want to sit. I don't want to sit *with you*."

"Trudy, I don't bite." Dan reminded himself to see things from Trudy's point of view. He'd broken Meg's heart once. And he knew Trudy took the care of Meg's heart very seriously.

He did too. Now, he needed to make the only real mother Meg had ever known understand that.

"Please, Trudy. I owe you an apology. If you can just give me five minutes, I'll say what I need to say, and then I'll go. You'll never have to talk to me again if you don't want to."

Trudy sized him up with an upward glance, followed quickly by a downward one. "Fine. Pull that little table over so I can prop up my leg."

Dan did as he was told, and then helped settle her on the wobbly wooden swing. Once she was seated, Dan lowered himself on the swing. He looked out toward the street and kept his hands resting on his knees.

"I was wrong, Trudy."

"I know."

The complete assurance in the older woman's voice made Dan laugh in spite of himself. "Nothing ever got by you, did it?"

"Nope. I had you pegged from the beginning, Golden Boy."

Dan dipped his chin slightly. "I deserve that."

"So, what are you going to do about it? Apologies are just words unless you put actions behind them." Trudy shifted her position awkwardly, but made sure she was facing him. Dan knew a lot was riding on how he chose to answer this.

"I'm going to make it right." He didn't even have to hesitate. He knew that much in his heart. Dan would correct the mistakes he'd made. But Trudy asked for an action plan, not words. "I'm going to ask her to marry me again, Trudy."

The declaration should have shocked him.

But it didn't.

It felt totally right.

"Ellie needs a father who will be there for good," she said.

Dan reached out and took Trudy's hand. It half-surprised him that she didn't pull away.

"I didn't understand love when I was eighteen, Trudy. I thought I did." He looked her directly in the eye. He wanted Trudy to know he wasn't pulling any punches. "I've been a competitor my whole life. When I was younger, I thought winning was everything. I wanted to win at all costs, because that's what I'd been taught was the most important. But I've competed now at a lot of different levels—high school, college, the league...and now I'm seeing it all from the perspective of being a coach. Along the way, I've learned it's not the victories that teach you who you are. It's the losses—and I lost it all. I want to find it again."

"But what about what *they* lost, Dan?"

Trudy's words stuck in his mind like a dart puncturing the bullseye.

"I know I can't make up for that, Trudy. I can't. But we can move forward...together. Together as the family God meant us to be. Two years ago, I committed to taking my boys on the team to church. I've had the chance to listen to some great men of God in several churches here in Port Provident, and I recommitted my life to God about a year ago. I told Him I didn't want wins above all else. I wanted His plans above all else. My wife and my daughter returning to Port Provident isn't a coincidence. It's part of His plan for my life, for Meg's life, and for Ellie's life."

Trudy took a deep breath, then exhaled slowly. She gave Dan's hand a quick squeeze.

"'The fear of the Lord is the beginning of the beginning of wisdom,'" she said. "That's from Psalm 111. Be wise, Dan. Please. Those girls are my world."

Dan saw tears like diamonds shining in Trudy's eyes. He wasn't sure they weren't also trying to make an appearance in his own eyes.

"They're mine too, Trudy. For better or for worse."

He lifted her hand and kissed it on the back. He'd been waiting for Trudy's acceptance and blessing for almost half his life. Now to make good on his promise—to ask Meg to stay in Port Provident forever.

Chapter Six

THE WEEK HAD PASSED swiftly, but yet, it seemed *soooooooooooo* slow. Three luncheon catering gigs and a dinner event last night at Provident College had kept Meg in the kitchen for most of the week, plus yesterday afternoon she'd met with Ellie's teacher to get an update on how she was adjusting.

Miss Sanderson had said the meeting would only take fifteen minutes, so Meg hadn't asked Dan to join her. This week was circled in red on his calendar. It was the homecoming game, to be played against Port Provident's number one rival, the Mainland High School Lions. She hadn't wanted to distract him from all the game preparation.

But now as the minutes ticked away on Friday afternoon, she was kicking herself.

This co-parenting thing would only work if she didn't make decisions *for* Dan. She had to make decisions *with* Dan and to remember she wasn't a single parent anymore.

Meg sighed. There were so many lessons she still had to learn. Would she ever get it right?

One thing she knew for sure was that she'd missed Dan this week. It was the first week since returning from Port Provident where they hadn't really seen or talked to each other. For so long, she'd conditioned herself not to think of Dan, to flip past football games on the TV, to not see his eyes every time she looked at their daughter.

And then about two months back on Provident Island had undone all that.

It had undone her.

"Ellie, come on, let's go! We've gotta get to Dad's game or there won't be any place to sit. This is homecoming, kiddo. It's a big deal. Are you ready?"

"Coming, Mom!"

Meg heard Ellie's feet on the stairs and her heart felt full. These were the moments she'd hoped for so long ago when Dan swept her off her feet back when they were only kids themselves. It felt so amazing to know everything had come full circle.

"Eleanor...oh my goodness, where did you get that?"

Ellie stood at the bottom of the stairs in a Port Provident High School cheerleader uniform, complete with her hair in bouncy ringlets pulled back in a half-up-half-down hairstyle and topped with an oversized giant bow.

"Trudy got it for me. She said a girl she fostered a few years ago was a cheerleader. She worked last night and this morning on making it my size. Isn't it cool?"

"The coolest." Meg meant the compliment wholeheartedly. "Trudy, this is amazing. But I felt like you've been kind of suspicious of Dan being in Ellie's life—and mine. Have I been reading you wrong? I've been running on almost no sleep the last two weeks, so I guess it's possible."

"No, you didn't." Trudy walked slowly into the front room.

Meg anchored a hand on one hip. "So what changed?"

"Wisdom."

"Huh?" It was the most ineloquent thing she could have said, and Meg knew it. But she had no idea what Trudy meant.

"It wasn't wise for me to keep Ellie from her father. Now, go to the game. Your husband is waiting on you."

Meg raised an eyebrow. Trudy hadn't even liked calling Dan Meg's husband back when they were actually married. "Ex-husband. Are you feeling okay, Trudy? Really. Should we stay home?"

"I've never been better, Margaret." Trudy looked straight down the bridge of her nose.

"You're pulling out my legal name, Trudy?"

The right side of Trudy's mouth curved upwards. "Yes ma'am. Now, skedaddle before I use your middle name, too."

THE AIR SMELLED LIKE October, the sound of the marching band echoed for miles, and the Port Provident Pirates were clicking on all cylinders and steamrolling the Mainland Lions in the biggest game of their season.

Everything about tonight was perfect.

But it had nothing to do with anything he'd just taken to heart. It had everything to do with the ring he kept fingering in his left pocket. He'd proposed to Meg on homecoming. History was about to repeat itself and it just felt right.

He'd left Trudy's house yesterday and headed straight downtown to The Island Jewelry Box, a local store featuring jewelry handmade by local artisans. Melanie Black, the owner, helped him pick a ring that was slightly non-traditional. It featured a smoky blue topaz in the center of a swirl of diamonds. He picked it because the oversized central stone reminded him of Meg's eyes and the diamonds surrounding it evoked memories of the spray of the waves at Point Provident under the lighthouse.

Nothing about their relationship had been by the book.

The engagement ring he presented Meg needed to be as unique as their journey.

At halftime, Dan started to jog into the locker room with his team. Then he stopped.

Three of the Port Provident cheerleaders went to the rail by where Ellie stood. Jenna Lynn crooked a finger at Ellie and lifted her over. Dan stood, rooted to the turf, as he watched the cheerleaders take Ellie by the hand and lead her to the fifty-yard line where the rest of their squad had assembled for the halftime performance.

He looked back toward the stands. Meg lifted her phone high and tapped on it to video Ellie and her new mentors.

Dan wanted to bottle this moment and hold on to it forever.

He put his hand in his pocket and touched the ring.

Forever was not far away.

"Hey, Coach! You coming?"

"Yeah, Chris. Let's do this." He took off jogging as the quarterback passed by. "All of it."

THE CLOCK WOUND DOWN.
  0:03
  0:02

0:01

Students leapt from their seats in the stands all across Pirate Stadium as Port Provident shut out their long-time rivals with a score of 42-0.

The game plan put together by Dan and the other coaches had been perfect. They'd adopted a hurry-up, no-huddle offense and it left the Lion defenders completely gassed. The win made Meg feel like a teenager again, herself. Friday nights had never been this fun in Austin.

Dan took off running as zero appeared on the clock above the scoreboard. He sprinted like a defender was trying to keep him from scoring the game-winning touchdown.

Meg headed down the concrete stairs to the curved railing by the end zone.

It felt like she was rewinding time and re-living that first kiss after the football game so many years ago. She smiled at both the memory and the present.

Dan reached up his arms and Meg leaned down. He picked her up and swung her over the metal edging.

"Gotcha," he said.

Ellie ran full speed from the cheerleader area and bounced into Dan's side, tackling him and pushing them all slightly off-balance.

"Did you see me with the cheerleaders, Dad?" Her cheeks were rosy from both the fall air and excitement. "They said since I'm Coach Clark's daughter, I can cheer with them any time. Mom, this is the best place ever. They don't let fourth graders cheer back in Austin."

As Dan lowered her to the ground, Meg reached out and straightened Ellie's giant grosgrain bow. "I'm glad you had fun, sweetie."

"Can we just stay here forever?" In a blink, her eyes transformed and looked like a cocker spaniel begging for table scraps.

Meg started to answer, but Dan jumped in. "Actually, I wanted to talk to you about that."

"About staying in Port Provident?"

He nodded. "Yes. Staying. Here. Forever. Where you were meant to be. Where you and I were meant to be."

Dan dropped to one knee on the turf and pulled out something from his pocket. Flickers and tingles of adrenaline began to launch through her veins, then a flood of emotion like an avalanche swept through her entire body as she saw the lightly-colored blue stone, surrounded by small white diamonds.

"Meg, I can't make up for the time we've lost, but I can make the time we have going forward the best years of our lives. I want to love, honor, and cherish you like I promised you back when we were eighteen. Will you do me the honor of becoming Mrs. Daniel Clark—again?"

The promise of forever at homecoming just felt so right. It spoke to her heart in that small place that had stirred when Dan had kissed her at the lighthouse and she remembered the verse from Song of Solomon.

I have found the one my soul loves...a forever homecoming.

She looked at Dan, then she looked over at Ellie. Their almost-identical faces bore the same hopeful expression.

Just one word—the right word—could bring so much happiness to both of them.

Meg's gaze flickered across the crowd as she drank in the moment. She didn't want to forget any of the details, not even the small ones.

Then she saw one detail she didn't expect.

The one detail that brought back a memory she could never forget.

Meg knew her answer.

"No. I can't."

"MEG, YOU HAVE TO TALK to me." Dan chased Meg across the football field, tucking the ring in his pocket. "Meg, please. Stop. Wait."

Meg held Ellie's hand tightly and never slowed down.

Then Dan realized she was headed toward Lamont Brown.

And Lamont was talking to Barry Haynes.

Dan wanted to rage. Loudly. But he reminded himself that he needed to keep it together. Parents and students were everywhere. The homecoming game crowd had been at Pirate Stadium's capacity. And they'd all seen him get rejected on one knee.

But what was Barry Haynes doing here? He'd given specific instructions to Zack to make it clear that Barry was *persona non grata* in every part of the Pirate football program.

Dan scanned the crowd. Zack stood with a group of players, but he was too far away for Dan to get to right now. This had to be made right.

Right now.

"Get away from him, Barry." Meg's voice could have cut glass.

Dan's fingers rubbed the diamonds in his pocket.

"Well, Meg. Long time, no see. I'm just helping Lamont out with some projects related to his college recruitment."

"No, you're not." Meg's reply left no room for questions.

Barry reached out and put a hand on Lamont's shoulder. "I'm helping him gather some film for his video to send out to collegiate coaching staffs. Lamont has a bright future ahead of him in Division One football. How do you know Lamont?"

Meg wasn't tall, stature-wise, but she squared her shoulders and took Barry on. "I'm his sister."

Barry laughed.

"Shut up, Barry," she said. "Lamont's foster mother is my aunt. Trudy has the legal authority to make decisions on Lamont's behalf, and I will see to it that you are not allowed to contact him ever again. If he needs film for his recruitment, I'll find someone to take care of it. Someone other than you. You're a liar and a cheat and Dan may be okay with you in his life and his program, but I'm not okay with you anywhere near mine or those I have some responsibility for. Come on, Lamont. We're going home."

Meg reached out her free hand to Lamont and tugged on his forearm.

Then she spun around and looked Dan straight in the eye. All Dan could see was fire—an all-consuming fire.

"You lied to me, Dan."

There wasn't any use in arguing. He could have explained that he delegated the contact to his assistant coach. But it wouldn't really matter. This was his football program. He was the head coach at Port Provident High School. The buck stopped with him.

"Meg, I'm sorry. I thought it was done. He's not welcome here. I promised you that, and I meant it. But I didn't follow through with Zack to make sure the message was delivered."

"It seems like you rely too much on others to deliver messages in your life, Dan."

And with that damning proclamation, Meg walked past Dan. Ellie shuffled along on one side, and Lamont followed a half-step behind on the other.

Dan's heart followed in their wake. He knew he'd never be whole again.

THE ONLY THING ELLIE wanted for Christmas was to see the Port Provident Pirates play in the Texas state football championship game. After Ellie and Meg returned to Austin, Ellie followed the adventures of Friday night lights online. Ellie even asked her mother to get a subscription to the local newspaper so she could read coverage of games across the state.

In just a matter of months, she'd completely become her father's daughter.

And it killed Meg to know that the three of them would never be the family Ellie deserved.

But, Meg knew Ellie also deserved to be able to think the best of her dad, so Meg subscribed to the paper and sat through recaps of game highlights on the ten o'clock news. It was the least she could do.

It was the only thing she could do.

Because never again would Meg lose her heart to Dan Clark. Twice had been enough.

"Mom!" Ellie came running into the living room. "I got an email from Dad! He's going to leave us two tickets for the championship game!"

"Isn't it in Dallas, Ell?"

Her daughter's eyes sparkled like stars. "Yeah. At Cowboys Stadium. Isn't it amazing? Dad and the guys are going to get to play where the Dallas Cowboys play. Isn't that so cool, Mom? We've gotta be there."

Meg mustered a smile. "Yeah, kiddo it is cool. It's been a while since Dad played in an NFL stadium. I'm sure he'll enjoy it."

"Do you think Jenna Lynn and the other cheerleaders would let me cheer with them?"

Meg bit her lip.

"Mom? Do you?"

"I'm sorry, kiddo. What?"

"Do you think the cheerleaders would let me cheer with them?"

It seemed like a foregone conclusion to Ellie that they'd be going. "I don't know what all the rules would be on that, Sweetie. But I'm sure that if they're able to do it, they'd let you. They loved having you on the field with them back in Port Provident."

Ellie played with the end of her ponytail. "Will we be able to go back to some games next season in Port Provident?"

Meg took in a deep breath. She didn't ever want to return to Port Provident, but she knew that for Ellie's sake, she had to remain committed to co-parenting with Dan. "That's a long way off. Maybe you can go visit your dad for a weekend or two."

"But we can go see him next weekend, now that they made it to the finals and he's giving us tickets. That'll be so cool."

Meg could think of about twenty-seven other words to describe seeing Dan again, even from afar. Thank goodness Cowboys Stadium could hold about a hundred thousand people. It meant that no matter where their seats were, there would be plenty of distance between her and Dan. She'd leave the binoculars at home.

She'd leave her heart there, too. Maybe a four-hour drive between Austin and the stadium would be enough distance to keep it safe.

DAN SAW THE LITTLE streak of lightning running toward him. He scooped Ellie up in his arms as soon as she launched toward him. Her all-access pass swung back-and-forth around her neck.

"Hey there, Ellie Bug!" He tried not to squeeze too hard, but he hadn't seen her in more than six weeks. He'd missed the first nine years of her life, but missing the past month and a half seemed to hurt the most of all. Now he knew what the hole in his life was.

Dan placed Ellie back down and looked up. The other half of the hole in his life stood a respectful distance back from the father-daughter reunion.

"Meg." Dan nodded slightly. He didn't know what else to say. Everything about Meg's body language said she was not looking for small talk.

She had driven a long way to bring their daughter to see him. That counted for something. He'd respect that and follow her lead.

Even if it meant not talking to her.

Even if it meant not asking once again for her forgiveness.

Even if it threatened to pull apart his heart, leaving him to bleed out at one of the NFL's premier stadiums.

"Hey, Ellie Bug... I've got to go do an interview with the Texas Sports Network. Do you want to come with me?"

The oversized bow atop Ellie's head bounced in reply. "You're gonna be on TV, Dad?"

"Yup."

"Way cool."

"It should only take about ten minutes," Dan said, raising his voice to be heard across the corridor. "You're welcome to come too, Meg."

Her ponytail bounced as she gave a non-plussed shrug and took a step forward. "Okay."

The slight Texan accent curled around his ear. Meg had only given him one syllable, but that was a start.

Dan followed the Texas Sports Network staffer to their on-site studio. He held Ellie's hand the whole way, and Meg kept a distance of a few steps behind.

As they stepped in the studio, Eddie Peak, the lead anchor for the network's coverage of the Texas high school football championships, put out his hand toward Dan. "Coach

Clark—it's great to have you join us today. Thanks for making time before the game."

Dan shook Eddie's hand. They'd done several interviews throughout the course of Dan's career. "I appreciate you letting me have the opportunity to speak. The Coaches' League and I are making this a priority."

"Well, let's get started so we don't take you away from game prep any longer. You can have a seat in that chair right there, and we'll get started."

One staffer clipped a lapel microphone on the collar of Dan's blue knit shirt, just above the Port Provident Pirates embroidered logo. Another gave him a quick touch of powder to make his skin not so reflective under the hot studio lights. Within a few minutes, the cameras were ready to roll.

"Welcome back to Texas Sports Network's coverage of the Texas High School Football Championships. Tonight's game is between the Port Provident Pirates and the Blue Creek Panthers for the Class Two division title. We have Head Coach Dan Clark of the Port Provident Pirates with us for a few minutes. Coach Clark is also the incoming president of the High School Football Coaches' League of Texas—and a Texas high school and college football playing legend himself. Coach Clark, welcome to this special live edition of Texas Sports Report."

Dan could see Meg leaning against a wall of the studio, her arms crossed. He wanted to study her face as he laid out the Coaches' League's new initiative. She'd driven the change, she just didn't know it.

He was doing this because it was the right thing to do.

But he was also doing it for Meg.

If he could make a difference for the better in the lives of student-athletes across the state, it would be the apology he knew he'd never be able to give her in person.

Apologies are just words unless you put actions behind them.

Trudy's words had been a challenge to him in the weeks since Meg left town. They spun in his mind like a tightly-thrown football headed for the end zone. He knew his carelessness in turning Barry over to Zack to handle had cost him dearly.

He had no one to blame but himself.

And no one could make it right but him. He wouldn't delegate any more. It would be his voice delivering this message loud and clear on TV to everyone who followed or was a part of Texas high school football. They'd all know exactly where Dan Clark stood on this issue.

"Thanks, Eddie. I'm glad to be here. It's my favorite time of year—championship week. The competition at all levels of football here in Texas is unlike anywhere else. And the Coaches' League wants to make sure we preserve the integrity of the sport."

Eddie gestured at the replica of the trophy awarded by the state athletics committee to the winners of the various championship games that would be played this week. "It's fair to say that football isn't just a beloved pastime in this state—it's big business."

"That is absolutely correct, Eddie. And as we've seen a rise in the recruiting services that track these athletes as they go through high school and are recruited by colleges all over this country, we've seen a rise in third parties who offer services to athletes in the hope of making them stand out to coaches at the next level. It's becoming a concern to me and to other coaches that some of these third parties are trying to act as *de-facto* agents, which is illegal, according to the bylaws of both our state athletics governing body and that at the university level. And so, today, on behalf of my fellow coaches across the state, I'm announcing our new Winning with Integrity program, designed to vet who we as coaches will allow near our programs. We want to put more formal systems in place so that our student-athletes and their parents can feel more confident in navigating the maze of recruitment that will hopefully take them to the next level."

Dan looked away from the camera for a split second, just to assess the look on Meg's face. Her jaw dropped slightly and she took two steps forward.

She knew exactly what he was talking about.

Dan was able to let out the breath he'd been holding deep inside. She knew. No matter what else happened between them, that was all that mattered.

He'd put his apology into an action, and hundreds—if not thousands—of kids across the state would benefit from the effects.

A wave of sadness washed over him as he realized that this initiative would benefit so many kids, except one. Ellie. Because no matter what he did going forward, Meg would never entertain the idea of bringing their family together again.

MEG NEEDED A MOMENT. She saw the sign for the restroom at the back of the studio area and quietly excused herself as soon as the red light that indicated filming in progress turned off. As soon as the door clicked shut behind her, she leaned up against it and tried to hold steady the quaking emotion in her chest.

Dan had delivered this message himself, and he'd delivered it loud and clear.

The days of people like Barry Haynes were numbered. Not just in Dan's sphere of influence—but all across Texas. And perhaps, one day soon, even beyond the borders of the Lone Star State.

The ball had been passed to her.

What play would she call?

Meg couldn't stay in the small bathroom forever. And she knew she couldn't carry this resentment toward Dan around forever, either. She closed her eyes and remembered how free she'd felt in Port Provident the night she forgave Dan. She argued with herself. She had forgiven him that night for all those years before. But this was different. It was a different time, a different action.

Except that really wasn't, and she knew it.

She'd been so quick to storm off the Pirate Stadium field because of how the past connected to the present that night. So, didn't that just mean she really hadn't forgiven Dan for the past? Or maybe she'd forgiven, but not forgotten.

How did that work, really, though? If she still carried the mistrust and the hurt in her memories, then she hadn't forgiven at all. She wasn't who she thought she was. She wasn't who she wanted to be.

She wanted to be free like that night under the lighthouse.

It wasn't enough to forgive, only to have her inability to forget jump up and snatch the hard-fought victory back from her hands and her heart when times turned bad.

What was she teaching Ellie?

On the day Ellie was born, Meg swore she would show her daughter unconditional love.

But her actions toward Dan demonstrated conditional love.

Love wasn't conditional. Trudy showed her that a long time ago. Ellie reinforced it. And her own belief in God told her it was true.

Meg knew now was the moment she truly needed to live what she knew in her heart.

"DAD, CAN I SIT WITH you?"

Butterflies still never failed to settle in Dan's stomach before a big game, even after all these years. But Ellie's joy in every aspect of being a part of this championship event grounded him.

He tapped her white bow. "You just want to go cheer with the girls, don't you?"

She giggled, and the sound filled his heart with warmth and love.

Meg hadn't said much since they left the studio area. Her brow seemed to stay in a permanent furrow. He'd hoped his words at the interview would have meant something to her, but he could also understand if the breach of trust revealed back at Pirate Stadium had just gone too deep.

It saddened him, but he knew he'd need to accept it. They'd always have a connection through Ellie. He knew that in spite of everything, Meg would honor her commitment to parenting Ellie alongside him.

It would have to be good enough.

They followed the official escort back to the tunnel so Dan could get back to the team's pre-game warm up on the field. As they stepped on the turf, Meg plucked the shoulder seam of Dan's shirt.

"Can I talk to you for just a minute, Dan?"

His pulse picked up several extra beats. "Um, sure, Meg. Ellie, it looks like the cheer squad is practicing in the corner. Why don't you go say hi?"

She ran off without needing any more prompting.

Even with all the pre-game noise surrounding them, Dan heard Meg's shaky breath as she inhaled deeply before beginning to speak. "What you said today...that will really help kids. It's a good thing."

"You were right, you know." Dan put the truth out there between them. "You always have been."

She shook her head. "No. No, I haven't."

"What do you mean?"

"I said I would trust you. I didn't."

"You had your reasons. I get it. I know how it looked."

She shook her head. "How it looked shouldn't have mattered. Things aren't always what they seem. I know that. You told me right then that you'd delegated it to Zack. I didn't want to believe you. I wanted to blame you."

"Meg, you don't have to do this." Dan wasn't about to be the cause of any more pain in Meg's life. He could live with a lot of things—even distance between them, if that's what she wanted. But he couldn't live with more pain between them.

"I do."

Dan swallowed hard. Not so long ago, he'd hoped to hear those words again from Meg as they undid the mistakes of the past...together.

"I just want you to know all of it wasn't for nothing. I hope it all was a catalyst for a greater good, even though it didn't work between us."

Meg looked Dan square in the eye. Her gaze was focused, steady. "Do you think it could, though?"

"What? Be a catalyst for good?"

"Work between us. Do you still want to try?"

Dan clamped down on the adrenaline in his veins. He struggled to stay in control of his feelings as he processed Meg's words. "Meg, there's nothing I wouldn't try for you. Or for Ellie. There's nothing—not even winning this game—that I want more."

She put out her hand and took his. "Me too."

Dan looked in Meg's eyes and saw trust riding back in on a wave like the ones that swirled below the lighthouse. He took her other hand and pulled her close and leaned down for a kiss that brought everything around them to a halt. There was no marching band, no cheer practice, no chirp of a whistle during drills.

Only him and Meg and a gateway to something that would stand the test of time.

"I love you, Meg McMahon," Dan whispered as he savored the last of the kiss.

"It's Meg Clark. Forever."

You Don't Have to Leave Port Provident!

Start Language of Love—the First Book in the Home to Love Series – Now!

GRACIE GARCIA'S MISSION has always been to help immigrants like herself, and with her English as a Second Language school, she is able to impact the Port Provident Community in a meaningful way. When real estate development plans pushed forward by Jake Peoples, a member of the island's most powerful family, threaten to shut down the school, Gracie hopes that getting Jake to attend a class will change his mind. But when a secret about Jake's past becomes the talk of Port Provident, he may not be able to save Gracie's school—or himself. Will love—the universal language—help Jake save her dream...and his place in her heart?

Publisher's Note: This book was originally published as Saving Gracie.

https://books2read.com/LanguageOfLoveBook

**Join Kristen's Reader Community Today and Receive a
Free Port Provident Story**

Join Kristen's reader community today for the latest and get A
Place to Find Love, *a sweet escape romance that introduces you
to Port Provident, Texas and the residents who find love on the
island, for free!*
www.kristenethridge.com/newsletter[1]

Sneak Peek: Language of Love—Chapter One

THE SUN'S LAZY DESCENT over the Gulf of Mexico began for the evening as Jake Peoples pulled the eviction notice from the glove compartment of his truck. Since he was already parked in front of El Centro por las Lenguas—which his rusty Spanish skills translated as "The Center for Languages"—it made the most sense to just serve the notice now.

The imminent passing of the Maximized Revenue Zones ordinance he'd shepherded through the City Council shortly after his return to town made Jake one step closer to convincing Port Provident that he could run his family's business. And once this building was demolished to make way for the sparkling pool to enhance the new Peoples Property Group condominium development, he'd be one step closer to convincing himself he wasn't the failure he had come to suspect he just might be.

When Jake turned the age-worn brass knob on the remodeled Victorian home's red front door, it didn't budge. Locked? No wonder this place was a nonprofit. He'd made mistakes in business, to be sure, but even he knew the first rule of running a company was you couldn't make money if the doors were closed.

He raised his fist and rapped on the solid wood.

After about thirty seconds of silence, the distinct sound of the lock turning broke through. A woman of average height stepped into the sliver of an opening.

"Can I help you?" Her brow furrowed across a forehead whose smooth complexion fell a shade lighter than the designer latte he'd polished off this morning.

Jake had faced judges, juries and his own father. He could easily face a schoolteacher. "I need to speak to Gracie Garcia."

"I'm Graciela Garcia de Piedra." Her consonants rolled together with a south-of-the-border accent.

"Jake Peoples." He extended his hand. "Peoples Property Group."

Instead of reaching to shake, her hands flew up and cupped over her mouth. The combination of the vulnerable reaction, combined with the oversized door, further dwarfed her stature. She looked as if she might blow away in a strong gulf breeze. "Oh no... I know the rent check was a few days late this month. It's been tight lately. I'm so sorry. It won't happen again."

The shock in her voice reverberated on his eardrums. Jake thought of the eviction notice waiting in his back pocket. She might have fainted if he'd held it out to her as soon as she opened the door. "I'm not here about that. I need to discuss the City Council's Maximized Revenue Zones proposal with you."

"I don't know what you're talking about, Mr. Peoples." The questioning wrinkles returned above the pair of liquid-chocolate eyes. "I teach classes at the same time as the City Council meetings, so I never have the opportunity to attend them. I know there are condominiums being put up next door, but I assumed they would be confined to that large corner lot they're already working on."

He shook his head briefly. Jake needed to break the gaze between them if he wanted to maintain his concentration. Gracie Garcia had the kind of dark eyes that a man—even a landlord here on business—could lose himself in. In his former career as a lawyer, no member of a jury pool ever gave him a stare that shook him like this.

"The City Council will soon be rezoning Gulfview Boulevard to make the most out of the areas in town that cater to our tourist-based economy. Nonprofit businesses, like yours, will need to move to new locations outside these zones. This property will be needed so we can add amenities like a swimming pool and a clubhouse, which will allow us to sell more units and, in turn, direct more tax dollars to the city."

"You're saying I need to close?"

Was there a language barrier between them? Maybe he'd gotten the wrong contact name. Maybe the woman with the magnetic stare was a student, not the owner. The name she'd given was a lot longer than just plain old Gracie Garcia.

"I didn't say anything about closing. Just moving."

"With all due respect, it's not that simple. I'm a nonprofit organization. I operate on a nonprofit's shoestring budget. If the council forces El Centro to relocate, I'll have to close my doors."

Well, she was certainly talking like the owner. Absently, he wondered why she gave a different name.

"Surely you can find additional funding. The Houston newspaper just did a story last week on unused grant money."

The woman nodded her head in understanding. Her eyes glazed over with sadness, but she didn't back down. She had guts; Jake had to give her that.

He didn't particularly like that his words hurt her, but he couldn't afford to get caught up in the emotions. This vote was nothing more than a necessary step in a business plan. Above all, Jake knew he had to remember why he'd come home to Port Provident in the first place. No more "bleeding heart" stuff, as his father used to derisively refer to Jake's past endeavors. Emotions and business did not make a successful combination, and Jake had returned to Port Provident to take steps at Peoples Property Group that would ultimately prove to a generation of naysayers that he could be successful.

"Can I come in for a few minutes so we can discuss this?" At least he would try to honor the promise he'd made to his friend sponsoring the ordinance, City Councilman Carter Porter. The City Council temporarily postponed their vote until affected businesses could be notified and given a chance to adapt. By meeting the owner of El Centro personally right now, Jake could report back to Carter that the box had been checked. That way there could be no more delays.

She shook her head. "You've caught me at a bad time. I have a class tonight that I need to finish preparing for."

"Okay, Ms. Garcia. Best of luck with your school. Here's the official lease termination paperwork, which will be effective once the City Council passes the measure at their next meeting." He reached in his back pocket and pulled out the document, then something made him pause.

Jake couldn't get the name discrepancy out of his head. He needed to be sure he'd just lowered the boom on the right person. It wouldn't look good if he'd delivered the message to someone else by mistake. "You are the owner of this school, right? You're Gracie Garcia?"

She nodded. "Yes, why?"

"I thought you'd said something else a few minutes ago. Wasn't your last name longer?"

"My name is Graciela Garcia de Piedra. In the Mexican culture, children often have the surnames of both parents. The father's surname comes first, and then the mother's—but children go by their father's last name. So I go by Garcia. It makes things simpler. Do you know much about our culture and language, Mr. Peoples?"

"No." He raked his free hand through his hair. "I'm afraid I don't."

"Then maybe you don't understand just why this school is important and what the impact is of what the City Council is trying to do," Gracie said with a soft, yet deliberate clip to each syllable of her quiet words. She took the offending paperwork from Jake's hand, then slowly closed the door. The rasp of the turning lock brought a clear end to their encounter.

Jake turned to head back to his car, feeling uncomfortable about the message he'd just delivered, even though he knew he had no other option. The passage of the City Council resolution was key to finalizing Port Provident's newest condo development. The project was key to his remaining at the helm of Peoples Property Group. And remaining CEO of his family company was key to restoring his reputation in his hometown.

The less time he spent at El Centro por las Lenguas, the better. His grandmother was being honored at a Port Provident Historical Society dinner this evening, and he didn't want to miss her big night.

As he pushed the button that unlocked the truck's doors, he heard the crunch of gravel under feet behind him. Two fingers tapped lightly on his shoulder. Jake turned and saw Gracie's eyes first, silently pleading with him. Her pupils flared wide, crowding out the brown velvet coloring. He could see the fear within.

He hoped she couldn't see fear in his own eyes. Fear that the City Council wouldn't give him what he needed to just get on with his life and not feel the cloud of failure hanging heavily on his shoulders.

"You said you didn't know much about my students and their heritage—where they come from and why they're here. More than three hundred members of this community have come through my doors in the last five years to better their English skills. I don't provide the city with tax dollars myself, but my students do make an impact every day." Her voice halted.

Jake turned. The gulf breeze gently stirred her hair around to caress her cheek. It appeared to be almost the same deep color as her eyes.

"The ordinance is passing in a few days' time. I'm not a City Council member. I can't stop them from voting on it," he said. "The measure would have passed today except that your representative wanted to give you some time to find an alternate arrangement."

"You said this proposal will maximize revenue for the tourist sector of our local economy, right?" Her eyes locked straight on his, like a magnet pulling to a pole.

"That's the goal, yes," Jake nodded.

"Many of my students work in tourist-related jobs, such as our hotels and restaurants. A skilled labor force is just as important to our city as tax revenue. I believe we can't have the latter without the former. Can you stay for my class in half an hour and see for yourself what I do here?"

Giving Gracie a few more minutes wasn't going to change anything, but it would probably make everyone involved feel as if he'd done his due diligence. It might also alleviate the nagging feeling in the back of his mind that something about what he'd told Gracie Garcia just wasn't right. But family duty called.

"I already have plans for this evening, Ms. Garcia."

"Then I'm afraid you won't see what a big mistake you're making for the citizens of this community until it's too late." Gracie headed back toward the center. She had some pluck. He recognized it because he used to have some, too.

Back before he lost everything.

When the City Council met next week and the inevitable happened, Jake hoped that Gracie didn't lose the determined spring in her step. The world didn't need another jaded former business owner.

BEFORE JAKE COULD OPEN the door to get back in the truck, his cell phone rang. "Jake Peoples."

"Jake, it's Mitch." The wind whipping up over the nearby water made it a little difficult to hear his brother-in-law's voice. "Where are you? Jenna's panicking."

"Tell Jenna I'm on my way. I'm just wrapping up a meeting."

"Who are you meeting with?" After meeting Jake's sister Jenna in college and marrying her, Mitch Carson joined Peoples Property Group and now served as the chief financial officer. Jake had much to prove to others at the office, but not

Mitch. His brother-in-law was doing everything he could to help Jake during this transition.

"Graciela Garcia de Piedra. She owns the school located in the building at Nineteenth and Gulfview."

"Oh, you mean the rental property you want to tear down so the new condos will have a pool that'll compete better with Goodman's new project?"

"That's the one. Just making sure that the council vote can go forward. I figured it was best to get it out of the way ASAP."

"Hey, wasn't her rent late again this month? If she's that disorganized, maybe you're doing her a favor. She'd probably go out of business anyway." Mitch chuckled. "Your sister just walked up. We'll see you when you get here."

"Bye."

The phone call disconnected, and Jake couldn't help but think about Mitch's last sardonic statement. Mitch was right. Gracie obviously had some issues running her business. Better that she quit while she could instead of being forced into bankruptcy. The way Port Provident's economy kept growing, she could easily find another job—a real job with a steady paycheck—in no time.

Jake saw two people headed toward him. Neither one was Gracie, but he felt certain he'd seen both of these individuals before.

"Mr. Jake?" The first man regarded Jake skeptically and stopped in his tracks about ten feet away. "Can we help you? Is something wrong at one of the buildings?"

Jake hesitated to answer. "No, no problem with any of the buildings,"

"Oh, good, sir. Juan and me, well, we weren't sure why you'd be at *El Centro* unless you were looking for someone."

Juan. Jake nodded his head with dawning recognition. The man on the left was Juan Calderon, the head of landscaping for Peoples Property Group. And the one speaking to Jake was Pablo Morales, head of maintenance.

"I had a meeting with the owner of the school. Just taking care of some business. Enjoy your class tonight." He opened the door to his truck and climbed inside as his two employees headed for the door of the school. Jake wondered what they'd say to Gracie when they got inside, but he knew he had nothing to hide about his motives for being here.

GRACIE PLAYED HIDE-and-seek as she placed two fingers between a couple of slats of the mini-blinds covering the window in her office. Through the space she'd created, she could search the parking lot without being seen herself.

She knew of the Peoples family's reputation in Port Provident, but Jake himself didn't look that tough. With sandy blond hair and square shoulders, he looked less like a hard-edged executive and more like one of the surfers who hung out down by the Memorial Hotel waiting to catch a wave.

"Is he still out there?" Her sister Gloria's whisper brought more reminders of childhood, when they shared secrets in hushed tones.

The parking lot had begun to fill for the evening's classes and Gracie could see the vehicles of several regular students. The truck that had parked in the very first space, however, had already left, leaving behind a trail that seemed to perfectly illustrate Gracie's dreams for her school—a cloud of dust, disappearing into nothing.

"No, he's gone."

"People like him make me so mad," Gloria said through gritted teeth. "Remember when you used to date David and he tried to stop you from opening this school? Now, here's another mover and shaker in the community trying to push you around. They're all the same on that side of the tracks. They'll do whatever they want and not care about people like us."

Gracie didn't want to remember the past, but Gloria was right. "Ugh. Don't remind me. Why is running a business such a constant battle? I'm trying to help people live their dreams, the way Miss Martin helped me so many years ago by teaching me English when we first came to America. She helped me to do everything I could to reach my potential. I just want to do the same for others. It shouldn't be this hard to do the right thing."

"Well, what are you going to do? I couldn't help but overhear." Gloria stopped arranging the evening's books and materials.

"I don't know, Gloria. How do I fight the City Council?" Gracie nibbled on the nail of her pointer finger, a sign of nervous thinking she'd had since childhood.

The sound of footsteps outside the open office door shook Gracie out of her stunned condition.

"City Council? Why don't you call Pastor Ruiz's aunt, Angela, for help? She's our representative." Pablo Morales stopped near where Gracie stood. "Remember, Juan, when she helped you with that property tax issue a few months ago?"

"Oh, *sí*. She got it fixed *muy rapido*. Only took one phone call. I still have her number right here." He pulled out a small black cell phone and punched a few buttons, then handed it to Gracie. "There. It's dialing."

Gracie tried to take a deep breath, but there wasn't any time. Angela Ruiz answered on the second ring. Gracie didn't even know where to begin. She still felt as though her world had been turned upside down. This building was her home and her school. And now she'd just received eviction papers, pending a City Council vote.

"Hi, Councilwoman Ruiz. This is Gracie Garcia at *El Centro por las Lenguas* on Gulfview Boulevard." She tried to force as much normalcy in her tone of voice as she could. "Jake Peoples from Peoples Property Group just stopped by and handed me an eviction notice, effective once the vote passes at the next meeting. Is this vote a foregone conclusion?"

"He did what?" The councilwoman's volume level escalated and Gracie had to pull the phone back from her ear. "Carter Porter assured me that Jake Peoples—your landlord—would work with you personally to make new arrangements. You were not supposed to be pushed out the door. I asked for the vote to be postponed out of respect for the work that you and a few other affected nonprofits do. Let me make a few phone calls. I'll be at *El Centro* as soon as I can."

The phone call disconnected, leaving Gracie as confused as before. Maybe when the councilwoman arrived, things would become clearer. But for now, she still had a class to teach. She walked the short distance from her office to the classroom.

"Okay, class. Let's get to work." She didn't completely know how she was going to take on the City Council and the leader of one of the city's oldest developers, but for the next hour, she knew she just had to focus on what she did best—teaching students.

A knock on the building's front door interrupted Gracie as she wrapped up the day's lesson. "Just a moment, class. Keep practicing your dialogues with your neighbor."

As she walked down the hall, trepidation gripped Gracie's heart. The last time she answered a knock at the door—only a few hours ago—she'd been unwillingly pushed onto the battlefield in order to save her school. What now?

"Hi, Gracie." Councilwoman Angela Ruiz stood on the front porch. Behind her stood a woman Gracie recognized—Patti Cortez, a local reporter from KPPT-TV. "I brought along a friend of mine. This wasn't what Carter Porter promised me would happen when I agreed to consider his proposal. I told him that he couldn't expect my vote unless the companies would help businesses like yours move to areas outside these new zones. And clearly, that's not happening."

Gracie stepped aside, speechless at Angela Ruiz's quickly marshaled support. "Come on in. I'm just finishing up a class, but you can wait in my office, if you'd like."

Angela and Patti stepped inside, followed by a cameraman. "I want to get a story on tonight's newscast. We need to let the people know this proposal is out there and let them tell their council members if they think it's a good idea or not. That's what good government is—the will of the people," said the councilwoman as she came inside.

Gracie saw a white van painted with the KPPT-TV logo in the middle of the parking lot, with a round satellite dish on a pole pointed at the sky. "Ms. Garcia, do you mind if my cameraman shoots some footage of you with your class? We can use it as B-roll in the story." The reporter poked her head around the corner and looked in the classroom.

This was really happening. El Centro would be on the news tonight. People all over Port Provident would be able to hear her plea for themselves. "If it's okay with my students, it's okay with me." Every head in the classroom was already turned toward the door. No more dialogues were being practiced. Clearly, everyone wanted to know what was going on. Angela Ruiz stepped in the room.

"*Holá*, everyone. Gracie and I need your help. There is a proposal in front of City Council right now that may mean the end of El Centro. I'm sure most of you have seen Patti Cortez on TV. If you'd like to be part of a story to help save businesses like El Centro, could you stay for a few minutes after class tonight?"

Heads nodded. The unanimous show of support bolstered Gracie's confidence, which had been plummeting ever since Jake Peoples showed up on her doorstep. She took a deep breath, as she exhaled, she smiled for the first time in hours. She'd always supported her students. Gratitude overwhelmed her as she realized they were supporting her in turn.

"Thank you, everyone. I'm going to step into my office for just a second while the TV crew sets up, and then we'll do this as quickly as possible." Gracie's words came straight from a grateful heart. "Councilwoman Ruiz, while we're waiting, could you give everyone an overview of what the proposal before the City Council is, exactly?"

Angela nodded and began to explain as Gracie retreated to the safety of her office to collect her thoughts. "What's going on out there, *hermana*?"

Gloria set a textbook down on Gracie's desk. "All of a sudden, everyone seemed to be talking at once." A midwife at the birth center near Provident Medical Center, Gloria was escaping from the hustle and bustle of the center and using the quiet of Gracie's office to prepare for some upcoming continuing education classes.

Gracie leaned against the closed office door and gave her nail a good, nervous chew. "I want to pinch myself, Gloria. A TV crew is here to do a story on saving *El Centro*. Angela Ruiz brought them."

"A story on the news—about *El Centro*? Well, that's nothing short of a miracle."

Gloria was right. The developers and council members supporting this crazy proposal would have to take notice. A smile began to work up the corners of Gracie's mouth. This felt like a plan, a concrete plan to show Jake Peoples just what *El Centro por las Lenguas* meant to real people in the Port Provident community.

Her school—her livelihood, her mission—would still be open until the City Council's next meeting. And in that time, she just had to show the man who actually owned her building that this proposal he supported was a bad idea, one that would cause Gracie to lose everything she'd worked years for.

"Jake Peoples and others like him who think nonprofits should just be moved off into a dusty corner need to see they're wrong. They need to see the faces of the people whose lives are changed by the work done by nonprofits." She could hear her voice becoming louder as her heart filled with passion for her school. "People who share the same dream Mamí and Papí had when they made the decision to come to America and give our whole family the chance at a better life. They sacrificed for me, and I want to repay that sacrifice by doing the same for others."

Gloria stood and gave her sister a hug. "Then you have to make the most of this opportunity. You have to let the people of Port Provident know why you matter."

Gracie knew the fight for *El Centro* promised to be a David-and-Goliath type of struggle. Thinking of it in those terms, though, made Gracie pause. It tempered her fighting spirit and scared her all over again.

She didn't have even a slingshot to wield. Jake Peoples was a BOP, local slang for "Born on Provident." Born on this island into one of the oldest families in town, he carried a birthright of privilege. And obviously members of the local government were just waiting to do his company's bidding.

When Gracie Garcia came into the world in a rural hospital in Mexico, she had a blue collar instead of a rattle. What was she thinking? In Port Provident, Texas, Jake Peoples wasn't just any man, he held a pedigree of royalty.

How could a working-class woman change the heart of a king?

"*Lo necesito...*" Gracie said, her voice barely over a whisper.

"What do you need, *hermana*?"

"I don't know, Gloria. I need..." Air rushed from Gracie's lungs in fear as she faced the reality ahead. She'd never been on TV before. She'd never had her home and livelihood threatened like this before. How could she do the work that needed to be done when she didn't even know where to begin?

"You need prayer." Gloria stood and walked to her sister, then took her hand and held on tight as she began to speak.

Gracie felt taller and stronger as her sister's words poured over her. "Thank you. I feel as if maybe I can fight this battle. You've made me feel as if I'm not in this alone."

"You're not, *hermana*." Gloria still held tightly to her sister's hand and squeezed again. "I've had your back since you were born, Graciela." Gloria placed an arm around Gracie's shoulders and squeezed. "*Somos familia*."

JAKE WALKED UP THE stairs at the Port Provident Garden Club, the scene of tonight's Historical Foundation awards dinner. He grimaced as he remembered being dragged to numerous functions here while growing up. Members of his family had been attending events at this place, the most exclusive club on the island, since it opened. Even so, Jake never felt as if he belonged here, because he never felt as if he belonged at any place that welcomed his father with open arms.

A chill ruffled the back of his neck, even though the weather felt like early summer. Jake never fully knew why his father's presence always made him uncomfortable, but at places like this, he still felt a nagging reminder of the icy coldness that had defined their father-son relationship.

Some things never changed, apparently. His father had died several months ago, but returning to Port Provident's most exclusive dinner club made a chill of self-doubt run down his spine, and he hadn't even run into a single person he knew yet.

"Jake!" Jenna waved her arms high above her head. Catching his eye, she waved him over to a table near the podium at the front. So much for his desire to lay low and not stir up any memories of his father in this old place. Slowly, he made his way to the space his sister had set aside for him.

Nana greeted him first, with a warm kiss on the cheek. "I'm so glad you were able to make it tonight, Jakey. Tonight wouldn't have been as special without you here."

"I wouldn't have missed your big evening for anything, Nana. You've done a lot of good work for a lot of people over the years through the Peoples Family Foundation. I am so proud to see your life's work recognized by this community." He admired how his grandmother used generosity and a giving spirit to make sure countless citizens had better lives.

"Jake...you're not going to believe this." Mitch grabbed his brother-in-law by the arm. "You've got to come with me."

"Mitch, what are you talking about?" Jake tried to make sense of why he was being led from the banquet hall like a show pony. "The dinner's about to start. Where are we going?"

"The lobby. There's a TV down there. You have to see what's on TV."

"But Mitch..." Jake's head spun, far beyond confused, as the pair walked down the stairs. "I don't even watch TV. You know that. I don't want to miss Nana's award."

His brother-in-law turned a corner, then stopped short, causing Jake to trip over his own feet. "You don't want to miss this, either." He pointed at the large TV on a pedestal in front of them both. Councilman Carter Porter also stood riveted to the screen.

Jake did a double take. On the screen was the same face framed by chocolate-brown hair he'd thought about during the entire drive to the Port Provident Garden Club. City Councilwoman Angela Ruiz flanked Gracie Garcia on the left, and the ESL teacher stood surrounded by at least fifteen other people. One held a sign. He locked his gaze on the words painted in red letters. "Save *El Centro*!"

"Turn the volume up." Jake's words came out sounding more like a bark than a request. He'd been wrong to question Mitch earlier. This definitely qualified as must-see-TV. It also qualified as the opening shot of a war over Gulfview Boulevard. How could Gracie have done this to him? He went to her school today to talk face-to-face. And this is how she repaid him? Public protests on a local newscast?

"Carter, what is going on here?" Jake spoke to his friend without looking in his direction. "I thought you said Angela Ruiz was onboard as long as I personally explained things to the owner of the school. I thought you were supposed to be helping me get through this."

"I am helping you, Jake. I brought your proposal before the City Council. I had enough votes lined up before Ruiz started asking questions. She's just new and trying to prove herself. Things will work out. Remember the district championship football game our senior year? You threw that pass with just a few seconds left. It started to pop out of my hands, but then I locked it down and ran it into the end zone." Carter clapped a palm of camaraderie on his former teammate's shoulder. "This is the same thing. We've been friends for a long time. I've never given up on you, even when you went to Austin. Don't worry, I'm going to score another touchdown with you on this one."

Carter's reminder reassured him. Gracie's little stunt would not keep him from the game-winning score Jake needed in order to ensure the success of the condominium project that would, in turn, ensure his confirmation as permanent CEO of Peoples Property Group.

This was now war. Gracie Garcia's students might be waving homemade signs of white posterboard on television tonight, but Jake promised himself that before the next City Council meeting, they would be waving the white flag.

Keep reading Language of Love

Click here:

https://books2read.com/LanguageOfLoveBook

The Holiday Hearts Series

The Right Resolution[1]
The Cupid Caper[2]
Lucky in Love[3]
May I Have This Dance[4]
First Kiss Fireworks[5]
Falling For Her First Love[6]
Thankful for Love[7]
Mission: Mistletoe[8]

Want to extend your stay in Port Provident?
Start reading the Hearts and Hope Series
Shelter from the Storm[9]
The Doctor's Unexpected Family[10]
His Texas Princess[11]

---

1. http://www.books2read.com/TheRightResolutionBook

2. http://www.books2read.com/TheCupidCaperBook

3. http://www.books2read.com/LuckyInLoveBook

4. http://www.books2read.com/MayIHaveThisDanceBook

5. http://www.books2read.com/FirstKissFireworksBook

6. https://books2read.com/FallingForHerFirstLoveBook

7. http://www.books2read.com/ThankfulForLoveBook

8. http://www.books2read.com/MissionMistletoeBook

9. http://www.books2read.com/ShelterFromTheStorm

10. http://www.books2read.com/TheDoctorsUnexpectedFamily

<u>Holiday of Hope</u>[12]
**Make Port Provident your home for sweet escape romance
with the award-nominated Home to Love Series**
<u>Language of Love</u>[13]
<u>Legacy of Love</u>[14]
<u>Labor of Love</u>[15]
Other Books by Kristen
Love Hallmark movies? Pick up Kristen's book October Kiss,
based on the Hallmark movie viewers love! Available
anywhere books are sold—in paperback, digital, and audio!
October Kiss from Hallmark Publishing[16]

---

11. http://www.books2read.com/HisTexasPrincess

12. http://www.books2read.com/HolidayOfHope

13. https://books2read.com/LanguageOfLoveBook

14. https://books2read.com/LegacyOfLoveBook

15. https://books2read.com/LaborOfLove

16. https://www.books2read.com/OctoberKiss

About Kristen

KRISTEN ETHRIDGE WRITES Sweet Escape Romance—stories with hope, heart and happily-ever-after—for Harlequin's Love Inspired line, Hallmark Publishing, and Laurel Lock Publishing. She's a Romance Writers of America Golden Heart Award nominee and both a Christian Fiction and Inspirational Romance #1 Best-Selling Author.

You can find Kristen in her native habitat—a Texas patio—where she's likely to be savoring the joy of a crispy taco, along with a glass of iced tea. Scents from her essential oil diffuser are also a must, since she's a certified aromatherapist. She's almost convinced her family that it's normal to talk to imaginary people, as long it goes in a book.

Find her online at http://www.kristenethridge.com where you can get a free story for signing up for her newsletter. You can also follow her adventures in writing at www.facebook.com/kristenethridgebooks[1].

Keep up with Kristen by joining her newsletter list[2] and her author pages on Bookbub[3] and Facebook[4]. If you can't get enough of Port Provident, come join the Port Provident Community Center[5] on Facebook, the official gathering place for Kristen and her fans.

<u>www.kristenethridge.com</u>[6]
<u>Facebook</u>[7] <u>Instagram</u>[8]
<u>The Port Provident Community</u>[9] <u>Center</u>
Don't forget…if you love sweet escape romances, join Kristen's newsletter[10]!

---

1.   http://www.facebook.com/kristenethridgebooks

2.   http://www.kristenethridge.com/newsletter

3.   https://www.bookbub.com/authors/kristen-ethridge

4.   http://www.facebook.com/kristenethridgebooks

5.   https://www.facebook.com/groups/2422381554654795

6. http://www.kristenethridge.com

7. https://www.facebook.com/KristenEthridgeBooks

8. https://instagram.com/kristenethridge

9. https://www.facebook.com/groups/2422381554654795

10. http://www.kristenethridge.com

Acknowledgements

To the SicEm365 community... Not only are you the best fan base ever, you are the best friends ever. Thank you seems inadequate, but it's all I've got, so thank you for pushing the ball across the line and getting me to Basalt. To my friends and family who also helped, I'm so grateful for your faith in me and your generosity. I love you all.

Oh, and to the Turnpike Troubadours...thanks for writing a song that's so stinking awesome that I couldn't get it out of my head until I wrote a story inspired by it.

"YES INDEED, IT WON'T be long now." God's Decree. "Things are going to happen so fast your head will swim, one thing fast on the heels of the other. You won't be able to keep up. Everything will be happening at once—and everywhere you look, blessings! Blessings like wine pouring off the mountains and hills. I'll make everything right again for my people Israel:

> 'They'll rebuild their ruined cities.
> They'll plant vineyards and drink good wine.
> They'll work their gardens and eat fresh vegetables.
> And I'll plant *them*, plant them on their own land.
> They'll never again be uprooted from the land I've given them."

God, your God, says so.'"

-AMOS 9:14-15 (MSG)

LAUREL LOCK PUBLISHING

Publisher's Note: This is a work of fiction. Names, characters, places, and incidents are a product of the author's imagination. Locales and public names are sometimes used for atmospheric purposes. Any resemblance to actual people, living or dead, or to businesses, companies, events, institutions, or locales is completely coincidental.

---

1.   http://www.zondervan.com/